YEARLING BOOKS/YOUNG YEARLINGS/YEARLING CLASSICS are designed especially to entertain and enlighten young people. Patricia Reilly Giff, consultant to this series, received the bachelor's degree from Marymount College. She holds the master's degree in history from St. John's University, and a Professional Diploma in Reading from Hofstra University. She was a teacher and reading consultant for many years, and is the author of numerous books for young readers.

For a complete listing of all Yearling titles, write to
Dell Readers Service, P.O. Box 1045,
South Holland, IL 60473.

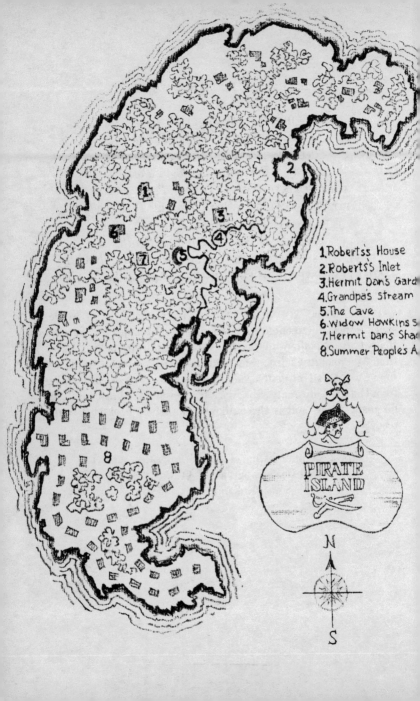

1. Roberts's House
2. Roberts's Inlet
3. Hermit Dan's Gard[en]
4. Grandpa's stream
5. The Cave
6. Widow Howkins s[ ]
7. Hermit Dan's Shac[k]
8. Summer People's A[ ]

PIRATE ISLAND

N
S

Pirate Island Adventure

by Peggy Parish

Illustrated by Paul Frame

A YEARLING BOOK

Published by
Dell Publishing
a division of
Bantam Doubleday Dell Publishing Group, Inc.
666 Fifth Avenue
New York, New York 10103

ISBN: 0-440-47394-2

Reprinted by arrangement with Macmillan Publishing Co., Inc.
Printed in the United States of America

February 1981

10 9 8

CW

For Annemarie Brown
and Caroline Clarke,
two of my favorite young
friends, with love

Contents

1

A Great Surprise

"Hey, the front door's open," said Bill. "Let's cut through the house."

"You know Mom keeps the screen door latched," said Liza.

"I'll race you to the back door," said Jed.

"I'm too tired," said Liza.

"But I think that's silly," said Bill.

"What's silly about being tired?" asked Jed.

"I didn't mean that," said Bill. "I mean keeping the screen door latched."

The children started walking around to the back.

"You know why she does that," said Liza.

"I do not," said Bill.

"Mom doesn't like surprises," said Liza.

"Surprises!" said Bill. "We're not surprises!"

"That's for sure," called Mom from the kitchen window. "But come in quickly. I have a real surprise for you."

"You baked cookies," said Bill. "I smell them."

"Yes," said Mom. "But that's not the surprise. Do hurry. It's long distance."

"Long distance!" said the children.

"It must be Gran and Grandpa," said Liza.

The children ran to the back door and into the kitchen. They tossed their books in a corner. Then they ran to the telephone.

"It's Gran," whispered Mom.

"Hey, Gran," said Bill. "Talk loudly. We're all here."

"Good," said Gran. "I guess I called a few minutes too early. I was sure you would be home by now."

"Is there any trouble about our coming this summer?" asked Liza.

Gran laughed and said, "I knew that would be your first thought."

"Well," said Jed, "it's just that you don't usually call at this time of day."

"I know," said Gran. "But we're kind of excited and couldn't wait to talk to you. Our plans have changed for the summer."

"Oh, no!" said the children.

"Just a minute," said Gran. "They still include you. We decided to go to the island. Grandpa has to see about getting a new caretaker. We would like for you to go with us. But we want you to think about it because it takes a couple of days of driving to get there."

"Think!" said Bill. "I don't care if it takes a week to drive. We want to go."

"It also means you'll have to miss the last three days of school," said Gran. "But your mother said that could be arranged."

"Hurray," said the children.

"Oh, and wait a minute," said Gran. "Grandpa wants to talk to you."

"Hello there," said Grandpa. "I just need to say one thing."

"We'll listen to you any time," said Liza.

"Tell your father not to go telling you any of my stories. I can do that myself," said Grandpa.

"Grandpa," said Jed, "what do you mean?"

"Never mind," said Grandpa. "Your father will know. Here's Gran again."

"I just wanted to tell you that Jelly Bean is going, too."

"Good," said Liza. "I can't wait to see him again. He was such a little puppy last summer."

"He's still little," said Gran, "and can get into just as much trouble."

"So can we," said Bill.

"Gran," said Jed. "Thank you for the nice surprise."

"Well," said Gran, "you all think about the long ride and talk with your parents. Then we'll make the final plans. This is a spur-of-the-moment thing. You know we usually go for Christmas."

"I don't know what we've got to think about," said Liza. "But I'm sure Mom and Dad will be talking to you."

"All right," said Gran. "Good-bye for now."

The children all said good-bye and hung up the telephone.

"The island!" said Jed. "I can't believe we are

finally going to get to go to Pirate Island."

"Gee," said Bill. "Suppose they don't mean Pirate Island? Nobody asked."

"Oh, don't be silly," said Liza. "That's the only island house they have."

"You think you know everything," said Bill.

"Oh, stop it," said Jed. "A really great surprise and you start squabbling."

"I can't believe it myself," said Mom. "Pirate Island at last."

"I wonder what Grandpa meant by not telling his stories?" asked Jed.

"Oh," squealed Liza. "I'll bet he's got another mystery for us!"

"Do you really think so?" asked Bill.

"You'll have to wait until your father comes," said Mom. "Maybe he'll know what Grandpa means."

"But that's hours," said Liza.

"I can't help it," said Mom. "We've waited years to go to Pirate Island."

"Oh," said Bill, "are you coming with us?"

"Not for the whole summer," said Mom. "But we'll come down for a while."

"So what do we do now until Dad comes?" asked Liza.

"I would suggest you have your snack and then get your studying done," said Mom.

"Snack!" said Bill. "Do you know I'd forgotten about that?"

"That," said Liza, "makes me believe in miracles."

2

Dad Arrives

The afternoon passed more quickly than the children expected. It was test time at school. There was a lot of studying to be done.

It was Bill who heard the car drive in. He shouted, "Hey, Dad's home."

All books were slammed shut. The three ran out to meet their father.

"Dad! Dad!" they called.

"Why all the excitement?" asked Dad.

"We've got great news," said Jed.

"Yes," said Liza and Bill together. Then all three children started talking. Dad laughed and put his hands over his ears.

"You sound like a gaggle of geese," he said. "Please, one at a time. You've really got me curious."

Liza took him by the hand. She said, "Come on in. We're too excited to take turns. Maybe Mom can help us."

"Okay," said Dad. "I'll race you to the door."

"You'll race us!" said Bill.

"I will," said Dad. "And I'll beat you, too."

They all started to run. Dad was right. He was in the kitchen before the others got to the door.

"Gee, Dad," said Bill, "I didn't know you could run like that."

"There're a lot of things you don't know yet," said Dad.

"You tell him, Dad," said Liza. "He won't listen to me."

"I could teach you a few things, too, young lady," said Dad.

"Hey, wait a minute," said Bill. "We hurried

so we could tell Dad the news, not have him read us a lecture."

"For once you're right," said Jed. "Where's Mom?"

"Mom," screamed Bill. "Where are you? We need you."

"I'm coming," said Mom. "And I'm not deaf. But a few more screams like that and I will be."

In just a minute Mom came into the kitchen. She said, "Now what is all the screaming about? Have you told Dad the news?"

"That's what we need you for," said Liza. "We're so excited we can't take turns."

"So start with the oldest and work down or start with the youngest and work up," said Mom.

"Oh, Mom!" said Liza. "You're no help at all. Dad, Gran and Grandpa are going to Pirate Island this summer."

"They are!" said Dad.

"Yes," said Bill. "And they're taking us with them."

"We even get to miss the last three days of school," said Jed. "And Jelly Bean is going, too."

Mom clapped her hands. She said, "See, you did it after all."

The children looked at each other in surprise.

"And we didn't interrupt each other once," said Liza.

"Well," said Dad, "that is some surprise. Now I have piles of questions to ask. See if you can keep on doing as well."

"We'll try," said Bill. "But it won't be easy."

"First, why are they going in the summer? Are the Fergusons going away?" asked Dad.

"Who are the Fergusons?" asked Bill.

"You know," said Liza. "The people who rent the house. They visit their children every year for the month of December. That's why Gran and Grandpa go there then."

"Oh, yeah, I forgot," said Bill.

"No, unfortunately old Mr. Ferguson died," said Mom. "Mrs. Ferguson has decided to go and live with her daughter. That's the main reason Gran and Grandpa are going now. They have to make arrangements about the house."

"I didn't know that," said Jed.

"No," said Mom. "You were too excited for me to tell you. Gran told me before you got into the house."

"I'm sorry about Mr. Ferguson," said Dad. "I

never knew him, but they say he was a very nice person and he loved the island. But I think it's great you three are getting to go."

"Mom wants to go, too," said Liza.

"Without me?" asked Dad.

"No, silly," said Mom. "For our vacation."

"That's a good idea," said Dad. "I have some extra time coming this year. We can have a nice long vacation."

"Oh," said Liza. "I just remembered something."

The others looked at Liza.

"You know," said Liza. "What Grandpa said."

"Oh, yes," said Jed. "Grandpa said for you not to tell us his stories. He could do that. Do you know what he means?"

Dad thought for a minute. Then he threw back his head and laughed.

"What's so funny?" asked Bill.

"Your Grandpa," said Dad.

"Do you know what he means?" asked Jed.

"I do now," said Dad. "I had completely forgotten about it."

"Oh, come on, Dad," said Bill. "Tell us."

"Yes, Dad," said Liza. "Do tell us what he means."

"All right," said Dad. The three children looked at him eagerly. Dad began, "He means for me not to tell you the stories he told me about the island. He can do that himself."

"Oh, Dad," said Liza. "You're horrible."

"Why?" asked Dad, "I told you what you asked."

"Does he mean a special story?" asked Jed.

"I think so," said Dad. "I'll tell you what I know about the island. But I've forgotten a lot. It's been years since I've been there."

"Why haven't you two gone?" asked Liza.

"Well, we got married when your father was in college," said Mom.

"And your mother worked to support us," said Dad. "Then right after college I started working."

"Gran and Grandpa had the house rented year round then, so they didn't go to the island either," said Mom.

"We spent our vacations either with my parents or with your mother's," said Dad.

"Then you came along, Jed," said Mom. "And before you were old enough to do much by yourself the other two showed up."

"And it takes a lot of money to support a family," said Dad.

"And a lot of work to care for three babies," said Mom.

"Then when the Fergusons took over the house and Gran and Grandpa started going in December, we couldn't get away. You know that's one of my busiest times at work," said Dad. "This is really the first chance we've had to go."

3

Plans Proceed

"Isn't there some way they could fly down?" asked Mom. "That's a lot of riding to do and they don't need the car on the island."

"That's a good idea," said Dad. "I hadn't even thought about it. I'm so used to their driving. But surely there must be an airport in Mainland. I'll call and see."

Dad went to the telephone. He called the airport and talked for a few minutes.

"Well," he said, "your mother had a good idea. You can fly there in just a few hours with only one change of planes."

"Do you think Grandpa will do it?" asked Jed. "He said one time he wanted nothing to do with flying."

"Yes," said Dad, "that might present a problem. But it's worth a try."

"But why wouldn't anybody want to fly?" asked Liza. "You get there so much quicker and I can't get to Pirate Island quick enough."

"We'll give it a try," said Dad. "I made the reservations anyway. Now we'll call them."

"Do you want me to get the number?" asked Mom.

"Yes, please," said Dad. "I want something to drink."

Mom dialed the number while Dad got a glass of lemonade. Then she handed the phone to him. He heard it ringing three times. Then Gran answered.

"Hi, Mom," said Dad. "Your phone call stirred up quite some excitement around here."

"We're excited, too," said Gran. "I'm so glad the children can go with us."

"We had to say yes," said Dad, "or we would

have had three runaways. Is it all right if Anne and I come down later in the summer?"

"Certainly," said Gran. "I just wish you could come for the whole time."

"So do we," said Dad. "And, Mother, I just called the airport. There's a good plane schedule that will take you right to Mainland. It only takes a few hours. Don't you think that would be better than driving?"

There was a long pause on the other end of the line. Then Gran said, "I think so. But I don't know if I can talk your father into it."

"Hey," said Bill. "I've got an idea. Let me speak to Gran."

"Bill needs to say something," said Dad. "He's about to explode."

Dad handed the phone to Bill. Bill said, "Gran, I just had an idea. If you have trouble talking Grandpa into flying, just tell him we are flying and will meet him there."

Everybody laughed as Bill handed the phone back to Dad.

"He might have an idea at that," said Gran. "I'll use it. Nothing else I've said has worked before. Oh, wait a minute. Here he comes now. He wants to talk to you."

"Hi, Pop," said Dad. "You have three curious grandchildren. They want to know what story you mean."

"You didn't tell them, did you?" asked Grandpa.

"Steal your thunder?" said Dad. "I wouldn't dare."

The men talked for a few minutes. Then Grandpa said, "Your mother wants to speak to you again."

"I forgot to ask you," said Gran. "We plan to

take the dog with us. Would that cause any problems?"

"Not at all," said Dad. "I went ahead and made the reservations. You see what you can do with Pop and let me know."

"All right," said Gran. "I'll start working on it tonight. Thank you for calling."

Dad hung up the phone. He said, "We'll see what happens now. I think Gran would really like to fly."

"Well, if we don't do some flying around here we're going to have no supper," said Mom. "Look at the time."

"I saw some hot dogs in the refrigerator," said Bill. "Let's have them."

"Yes," said Jed. "Let's have a celebration supper. Are there any potato chips?"

"Yes," said Mom. "And that's a good idea. Now everybody get busy. Make the salad, set the table, bring the hot dogs."

Nobody argued and soon everything was on the table.

"Dad," said Jed, "is Pirate Island all beach? Are there any trees?"

"Yes," said Dad. "There are lots of trees. Our

end of the island is more trees than beach. The other end of the island, which is quite a summer resort, is mostly beach."

"Are there stores and things?" asked Bill.

"No," said Dad. "A couple of days a week a motorboat comes over from Mainland and brings the islanders the orders they have phoned in. Of course in the summer there are boats every day."

"Do many people live there all the time?" asked Liza.

"Oh, a dozen or so, I think. Most of them are old-timers."

"What do you mean?" asked Jed.

"Well, they've been there for years and years. Their families have grown up and moved away. And no new people have moved onto the island. The children used to go to school in Mainland and they had to go by boat taxi. It was just too inconvenient. But there were too few children to have a school on the island. And until a few years ago there was no electricity or telephones."

"Gee, that sounds really primitive!" said Mom.

"It was," said Dad. "Primitive, but great. The old-timers didn't want what they called those modern fads. But the summer people outnumbered them."

"I'm glad for that," said Mom. "With no doctor on the island, they need telephones."

"Why don't Gran and Grandpa live there all the time?" asked Bill. "They seem to really love it."

"They keep talking about it," said Dad. "But remember their children and grandchildren are all here. I think that's what really stops them. You three are lucky. You are the oldest grandchildren. So you get to do everything first."

"Well," said Mom. "There are a few things you're going to have to do to get ready."

"What?" asked the children.

"Get out all your summer play clothes," said Mom. "Try them on and see if anything fits. Then we'll know what to buy. We really don't have much time."

"I think we can do that," said Bill. "Let's get started."

"Hey, hold it," said Mom. "I think something else comes first."

"Ah, the dishes," said Liza. "We were hoping you would forget."

"Never," said Mom.

"We should have thought about paper plates," said Bill.

"But you didn't," said Dad. "So get to it. Mom and I have to do some planning ourselves about what you need for the trip."

"Trip! That's the magic word," said Bill. "I'll even volunteer to wash."

"Yippee!" said Liza and Jed. They all clapped. Then Mom and Dad left the kitchen.

4

Time Draws Near

The next two weeks were hectic. The children had to finish taking their school tests, old clothes had to be tried on, and new clothes had to be bought. It was work for everyone. But finally that special Sunday came. Gran and Grandpa were due to arrive. The children kept watching the road.

"I see it! I see the car!" shouted Bill.

"Hurray!" shouted Liza and Jed. They ran across the lawn to the driveway. Grandpa stopped the car.

"Well, a greeting committee," he said. He and Gran got out. Everybody tried to hug everybody else at once. Jelly Bean yipped and bounced around them all.

"My," said Gran, "let me look at you. You seem to shoot up inches between every time I see you."

"Oh, it's really true," said Liza. "Gran and Grandpa are here. We're going to Pirate Island."

"Hi," called Dad. "Bring your grandparents on in. You're not going until tomorrow and your mother has supper ready."

"So early?" asked Liza.

"Well, we thought Gran and Grandpa would be hungry after their ride," said Dad.

"Early or not," said Bill, "I'm ready to eat."

"You always are," said Jed.

"Bill must take after me," said Grandpa. "I always seem to be ready to eat."

"Yep," said Bill. "Food is the magic word for Grandpa and me."

Everybody started into the house. Jelly Bean was snuggled contentedly in Liza's arms.

Gran and Grandpa washed up and everybody sat down for supper.

Mom said, "Gee, it's nice to see you. I don't

think I could have made it much longer with these excited children."

"To tell you the truth, we have gotten a little more excited each day ourselves," said Gran.

"I'm still not sure about this flying business," said Grandpa. "Do you really think it's a good idea?"

"I do it all the time for business," said Dad. "There's nothing to it."

"Oh, Grandpa," said Liza, "you'll love it."

"Well, I don't know," grumbled Grandpa. "I'm getting kind of old to be trying out these new kinds of things."

"I hope I never get that old," said Gran. "I was not too eager at first, but I'm looking forward to it now."

"Hurray for Gran," said the children.

"Come on, Grandpa," said Liza. "Do go ahead and tell us that story."

"What story?" asked Grandpa.

"You know, Grandpa," said Bill.

"Know what?" asked Grandpa.

"The story you told Dad not to tell us," said Jed.

"Oh, that," said Grandpa. He helped himself to some more beans.

"Do hurry, Grandpa!" said Liza. "We've waited so long."

"Yes," said Grandpa, "I guess you have. But you're going to have to wait until after supper."

"Grown-ups," said Bill. "They just don't understand about waiting."

Grandpa looked at the children. He said, "I guess you're right, Bill."

He pulled a piece of paper from his pocket. He said, "Here, this might start you thinking."

The children forgot about food. They took the paper. All three gathered around it.

"A bush with red flowers and some broken lines!" said Bill.

"What on earth does that mean?" asked Liza.

"I know!" said Jed. "It must be a new mystery."

"Is it, Grandpa? Is it a new mystery?" asked Liza.

"For you it is," said Grandpa. "For me, it's a very old one."

They waited for him to say more. But first he finished his supper. Then he said, "That was very good. I thank you, Anne."

"Will you tell us now?" asked Liza.

"I will," said Grandpa.

The children looked at their mother. She knew what they were thinking.

"Go ahead," she said. "This is special. I'll do the dishes."

"And I'll help," said Gran. "It will give us a chance for a good chat."

So Grandpa, Dad, the children and Jelly Bean went out on the lawn.

5

Grandpa's Story

Grandpa and Dad sat on lawn chairs. Liza, Bill and Jed sprawled on the grass around Grandpa.

"Well," said Grandpa, "I see you're all ready."

"And waiting," said Jed.

"So I'll begin," said Grandpa. "My brother was a lot older than my sister and me. And he was full of crazy ideas."

"Sounds just like you, Bill," said Liza.

"Oh, stop interrupting, Liza," said Bill. "I want to hear this story."

Grandpa went on. "Sometimes his ideas were really fun. But sometimes they landed all of us in trouble. This particular one got him in trouble with the whole family."

Grandpa chuckled. Then he shook his head.

"I can still picture the day we found out," he said. "This story really brings back memories. You see, my mother had her own ideas about children. We weren't allowed to take any toys to the island. There were only a few puzzles, books and some other things that stayed there. But my mother did believe in children learning how to do things. So we planned a project to do each summer."

"What did you plan that summer, Grandpa?" asked Jed.

"I'll come to that later," said Grandpa. "Let me finish the other part first. This is where my brother's idea comes in.

"We knew about my grandfather's treasure hunt, of course. We had all searched for the treasure," continued Grandpa.

"And then *we* found the key to the treasure," said Liza.

"Well, to get on, my brother decided to plan a treasure hunt for us. But he got things sort of backwards. Instead of giving us something, he took our finished projects. Then he hid them."

"But didn't you miss them?" asked Liza.

"No," said Grandpa. "We finished them a while before the summer was over. My mother believed in being ready to go days before it was time to leave. So she had helped us pack our projects to take home. My brother just watched. Then he took them back out. We were home before we found out about it. Then everybody set up a howl. He had even taken something from my father and mother."

"But, Grandpa," said Jed, "why did he wait like that? Why didn't he do it earlier so you would have a chance to find your treasure?"

"He wanted us to wait until the next summer. He thought it would mean more to us then," said Grandpa. "He thought the whole thing was terribly funny. But we sure didn't."

"What did he take of yours, Grandpa?" asked Bill.

"My ship model," said Grandpa.

"Ship model!" said Bill. "Did they have models when you were a little boy?"

"They sure did," said Grandpa. "Not the plastic kind you have. These were made from a soft wood. We had to cut the parts out with a razor blade. Then we had to sand them before we could use them. It was hard work and took a long time. I was so proud of mine."

Liza reached up and took Grandpa's hand. "What else did he take?" she said.

"My sister was just learning to do needlepoint," said Grandpa. "You know how much she loved to do embroidery and all kinds of sewing."

"Yes," said Liza. "She used to make all my party dresses when I was little."

"Well, that was the summer she started to really learn," said Grandpa. "My mother helped her to make a needlepoint bag."

"Maybe we should think of projects to do this summer," said Jed.

"Our project can be to find Grandpa's family's projects," said Bill.

Everybody laughed at Bill. Then Liza said, "What about your parents? What did they lose?"

"Wedding presents," said Grandpa.

"Wedding presents!" said Liza. "Why should they have wedding presents at the island?"

"These were very special presents," said Grandpa. "They never traveled without them.

You see, my uncle was a silversmith. As a wedding gift he made a very special pin for my mother. It had a silver frame. Inside the frame, under glass, was a piece of a blue butterfly's wing. It was beautiful. And my mother really loved it."

"Gee," said Liza. "I would like to see that. A real butterfly's wing in a pin."

"And what about your father?" said Bill.

"His gift was a belt buckle. It had a silver frame. The center was made with his initials. We knew it was a special occasion when he wore that buckle," said Grandpa.

The children were silent for a few minutes. They had to think about all of this. It seemed strange to hear Grandpa talking about being a little boy with a naughty big brother.

Then Bill thought of something. He said, "Grandpa, did your brother hide anything of his own?"

"He said he did," said Grandpa. "But he wouldn't tell us what. He said whoever found the treasure could have it."

"But why didn't you find the treasure the next summer?" asked Jed.

"Because we didn't get back to the island," said Grandpa. "A lot of things happened. It was many a year before I saw the island again."

"Didn't your brother ever tell you where he hid the things?" asked Jed.

"No," said Grandpa. "He would never do that. He just said they were in a safe place. But he did give us the first clue."

"He did?" said Liza. "What is it?"

"Is it in code?" said Bill.

"You'll have to decide that," said Grandpa.

The children looked puzzled.

"What do you mean?" said Jed.

"That was the first clue I gave you at supper," said Grandpa.

"But that was just a scraggly-looking bush with red flowers," said Bill.

"And some broken lines," said Liza.

"Does it mean anything to you, Grandpa?" asked Jed.

"Oh, yes," said Grandpa, "That bush was in back of the house."

"Is it still there?" asked Bill.

"I have no idea," said Grandpa. "I wouldn't recognize it without the flowers. It has never been in bloom when Gran and I went down for Christmases."

"But didn't you keep after your brother to tell you?" asked Bill. "I would have."

"That's for sure," said Jed.

"We did for a while," said Grandpa. "But time has a way of taking care of things. We just accepted our losses finally. Then I guess we forgot them. Taking you children with us to the island has brought it all back."

"Gee, Pop," said Dad. "I haven't heard you tell that story since I was a boy."

"I had to with your three," said Grandpa. "If they could solve my grandfather's puzzle, who knows but what they might manage this one? They're the first detectives our family has had."

"Well, their mother seems to need them now," said Dad. "She's on the porch calling."

The three children ran toward the house.

Off at Last

Everybody was up and scurrying around early the next morning. There seemed to be all sorts of last-minute things to do. But finally everything was done. The bags were in the station wagon and they were ready to go.

"Liza," said Gran, "did you and the boys check to be sure you had everything?"

"Yes," said Liza. "We double-checked."

"Okay," called Dad. "Come along. We've got to get moving."

They all piled into the station wagon.

Suddenly Mom thought of something. She said, "Jelly Bean! Where is Jelly Bean!"

Nobody knew.

"We'll find him," said Bill. The children got out and began to call the dog. They heard him yapping, but he didn't come.

"He's out back," said Jed. "Let's get him."

The children ran to the backyard. There they saw the little black dog looking up into a tree and barking.

"Oh, no!" said Liza. "I forgot the kittens. Who will feed them when Mom and Dad go away?" She ran and scooped Jelly Bean up. He squirmed to get down, but Liza held tight.

The boys looked up into the tree. They started laughing. Jed said, "He's done a good day's work treeing all three of the kittens at once."

"Don't worry," said Bill, "Mom will get someone to feed them."

"Well, that's it for Jelly Bean," said Liza. "I'm not letting him down until we're in the station wagon."

"We'd better hurry," said Bill.

The children ran back to join the rest of the family.

Gran looked at her watch. She said, "Why are we going so early? It's not that far to the airport, is it?"

"No," said Dad. "But we have to get the luggage checked. Then Jelly Bean has to be checked in at a different place. You people can have something to eat while I do that. I noticed very little breakfast was eaten by any of you this morning."

"We were too excited," said Bill. "But now that we're really on the way I am hungry. And I just can't wait to get on that plane."

"Well, I can," said Grandpa.

"It's not as dangerous as a car," said Dad.

Grandpa looked up. He said, "It's such a long way up there."

"But Grandpa," said Liza, "it's great. The clouds look like big banks of snow below you. The towns look like picture-book towns."

"Well, we'll see," said Grandpa. "I guess it can't hurt to try it once."

"Thank goodness you said that," said Gran. "Now I feel better about going. You were beginning to make me feel uneasy."

Soon they reached the airport and got everything taken care of. After he checked Jelly Bean, Dad joined the rest of the family for a cup of coffee. He said, "It won't be long now. They should be calling your flight number soon."

Dad was right. In about ten minutes they heard the call.

"Okay," said Bill. "That's us."

Quick good-byes were said and Gran, Grandpa and the children went to board the plane.

Gran and Grandpa both gripped the arms of their seats until they were aloft. Then they dared peek out the window. Both of them were fascinated with what they saw. Soon Liza, Jed and Bill got annoyed with them. They had so many questions they wanted to ask about the island. But Gran and Grandpa were too busy looking to answer. So the children finally gave up and began to read. Then the drone of the plane made all of them sleepy and they had a good nap.

The next thing they knew, they were landing.

"Where are we? Are we there?" asked Bill.

"Well, according to your father this is as far as this plane goes. Now we take a smaller plane that will take us to Mainland."

"Then how do we get to the island?" asked Bill.

"By boat taxi," said Gran. "That much I do know."

Soon the baggage was transferred. The plane wasn't crowded so the airline people let the children keep Jelly Bean in the cabin with them. It wasn't a long flight. It seemed as if they had just unfastened their seat belts aloft when the sign flashed on to fasten them for landing.

For a while after that it was chaos. The baggage had to be gotten to the docks. Then boat taxis had to be hired to take them to the island.

Finally family, baggage and puppy found themselves on a beautiful sunny beach. The next big task was to get the baggage to the house.

"Is it far away?" asked Jed.

"No," said Grandpa. "It's that big house set back in the trees. I just need a minute to look around and breathe the good air."

"Well, we've done that now," said Gran. "I would like to get this chore over so we can start enjoying our vacation. Jelly Bean, if you were bigger we would make you work, too. But you could help by staying from under our feet."

Jelly Bean was so excited by his first visit to the beach he kept darting among them and almost tripped them all. But everybody loaded up and started for the house. The children just couldn't believe it. They were on Pirate Island at last.

7

A Burglar or What?

"We're doing pretty well," said Grandpa. "One more load and we should have it all done."

"Could we have just a little rest in between?" asked Bill. "I must have packed this bag with rocks. It's so heavy."

"Me too," said Liza, puffing under her load.

But Jelly Bean wasn't puffing. He darted everywhere and investigated every bush along the way.

Gran laughed. She said, "He might be a year old now, but he is just as curious as ever."

Suddenly Liza stopped. She sniffed the air. She said, "I smell coffee and something else cooking."

"Nonsense," said Grandpa. "There's nobody close by here."

They walked on a little. Then everybody stopped.

"Liza is right," said Gran. "I smell coffee, too."

Everybody sniffed the air. Then Grandpa said, "And that other smell is bread baking. Now who in tarnation is in our house?"

"Are you sure you got the dates right, Grandpa?" asked Jed. "Maybe the other people haven't left yet."

"Of course I'm sure," said Grandpa. "They left a week ago."

"Maybe it's a burglar," said Bill. "Maybe he saw them leave and broke a window to get in."

"He wouldn't have to do that," said Grandpa. "There's no need to lock doors here. We don't even have a key for that house."

"Then he could have just walked in," said Jed.

"Either it's a burglar or a ghost," said Bill. "I think it's a burglar.

"Well, burglar or ghost, somebody is making coffee," said Jed.

"I don't care which it is right now," said Liza. "Somebody do something. I'm about to drop everything."

"Maybe I'd better investigate before we go on," said Grandpa. "Times have changed. Maybe somebody did decide to use the house."

"No! No!" said Liza. "Not by yourself. Something might happen to you."

The group walked a little farther.

"The front door is open," said Gran. "Somebody is surely there."

"I know," said Jed. "Let's slip around to the back. Then we can see who's in the kitchen."

"Great," said Bill. "Let's go."

They began to put things down.

"Now wait a minute," said Grandpa. "I'm not sure that's a good idea. Let's think about it."

"Don't worry about us," said Jed. "We learned to be as quiet as Indians in Scouts. Nobody will know we're there."

"I think we're making too much of this," said Gran. "The island is the safest place in the world. We'll just walk up to the front door and call."

"But, Gran," said Bill, "if it is a burglar, then he'll just run out the back door."

"That's fine with me," said Gran. "I don't wish to tangle with any burglar today or ever."

"And I'm with Gran," said Liza.

"But we've never had a chance to catch a real burglar before."

"Nevertheless," said Gran, "we're going to walk up to the front door just as we planned."

"Oh, all right," said the boys.

Everybody loaded up again. Jelly Bean was nowhere in sight. Burglars didn't worry him.

"At least I'm thankful we had a little rest," said Liza.

"I feel the same way," said Grandpa.

Soon they were near the front steps. Grandpa called. "Hey, is there anybody home?"

No one answered.

"See, I told you it was a burglar," said Bill. "Come on, Jed. Let's catch him out back."

"Oh no you don't," said Gran. She put her bags down and started up the front steps.

"Wait, Gran," said Grandpa. He hurried after her. The two walked up on the porch. Gran opened the front door and called, "We're here. Is there anybody in the house?"

"Coming, coming," said a voice.

"It sounds like a woman," said Bill.

Then the voice called, "Hello there. I didn't expect you so early."

"Mrs. Hawkins!" said Grandpa. "How good it is to see you."

"Indeed it is," said Gran.

"Your son sent me a telegram saying you would be in about lunch time," said Mrs. Hawkins. "I thought I'd have a little something ready for you. I knew you would be tired and hungry after the trip."

"That was very kind of you," said Gran.

Mrs. Hawkins looked at the children. She said, "And these are Jack's children. Jack was smaller than they are the last time I saw him."

The children were properly introduced. Then Liza said, "Jelly Bean! Where *is* Jelly Bean?"

Everybody looked around. No little black dog was in sight.

Mrs. Hawkins laughed. She said, "Don't worry. If you're looking for that little black puppy, he's in the kitchen. He's having his snack now."

"And boy, that's what I want to do," said Bill.

"Well, I have coffee, cocoa and fresh-made bread with plum jelly," said Mrs. Hawkins.

"Wow," said Bill. He took Mrs. Hawkins's hand and said, "Madam, I'm very pleased to meet you."

They went to the kitchen. In a few minutes everybody was eating. Gran and Grandpa chattered away, finding out about the island people they knew. The children were much too busy eating to talk. And then, too, they had other things to think about. The main thought was a scraggly bush with red flowers.

Finally they had had enough to eat. Liza said, "May we go exploring now?"

"No," said Gran. "First I want to show you your rooms and have you unpack a little. You will be too tired later on. I'll show you where the sheets are, too."

Gran let them pick their rooms. Each child had his own.

"Now," said Gran, "unpack. That shouldn't take long. Then you're free."

"May we go barefoot?" asked Bill.

"No, no," said Gran. "There are too many broken shells and things around. I don't want to spend the summer doctoring cut feet. Bare feet are for the water."

"Water! Swimming!" said Jed. "I had forgotten that. Can we go swimming, Gran?"

"If you can talk Grandpa into showing you the inlet we use. It's quite safe. But don't go off swimming just anywhere."

"Don't worry, Gran," said Bill. "We'll settle for our own inlet."

The children quickly unpacked. Then Liza said, "I'll go ask Grandpa about swimming."

She ran downstairs.

Islanders

Soon Liza was back. She said, "Grandpa will show us. Gran is going, too."

"Are they going to swim?" asked Jed. "Gran's a good swimmer."

"I think so," said Liza. "She went to change into her swimsuit."

"And that's just what I'm going to do," said Bill.

Soon the five were on their way to the inlet.

"I can't believe we can swim every day," said Liza.

"Do we have to have a grown-up with us every time?" asked Jed.

"Certainly not," said Grandpa. "You can look

after each other. You're all good swimmers. Of course, Gran and I might join you sometimes. But you don't have to wait for us."

The inlet was not far from the house. It was a large one and little waves lapped upon the beach.

"Oh," said Liza. "It's beautiful."

"It's hard to believe it's so calm when the ocean looks so rough," said Jed.

But Bill didn't say anything. He was already in the water.

"Hey, it's great," he called. "Come on in."

And that's just what the others did. In a little while the children stopped to watch Gran.

"Gee, Gran," said Liza. "I wish I could swim like you. It's just beautiful."

"Would you really like to learn my strokes?" asked Gran.

"Yes!" shouted all three children.

"All right," said Gran, "I'll teach you."

"When?" said Bill.

"First lesson right now," said Gran.

They worked for a short while. Then Gran declared she wanted some sun. Grandpa was already stretched out on a towel. He had been watching the lesson.

The children swam for a while longer. Then one by one they came out.

"Why does swimming always make you so hungry?" asked Bill.

"Everything makes *you* hungry," said Liza.

"No," said Bill. "I'm serious. I'm starving when I get through swimming."

"It's all that good exercise," said Grandpa. "But it should be getting close to supper time, anyway. Do we have any food, Gran?"

"Oh, yes, I arranged for food to be sent over," said Gran. "And that dear Widow Hawkins left the nicest cake for us."

"Widow Hawkins!" said Bill. "I thought she was just Mrs. Hawkins."

Grandpa laughed. He said, "You'll have to get used to that. Everybody here has some name people speak of them as."

"Really?" said Liza. "Who do you suppose we will be?"

"The people from the big house," said Grandpa.

"Well, Widow or Mrs. Hawkins, it's that cake I want. I'm like Bill now," said Jed. "I'm starving."

Everybody walked slowly back to the house. They were just too tired to hurry.

"In through the back door," said Gran. "There are towels there."

The children ran around back.

"Hey, what's that?" asked Liza. There was a package wrapped in newspaper on the back doorstep.

"What's what?" said Gran, as she came up to them.

"This package," said Bill.

"Now, I don't know," said Gran.

Grandpa chuckled. He said, "I'll bet I can guess."

"I'm not going to guess," said Gran, "I'm going to open it."

And that's just what she did. Then she exclaimed, "Fresh fish! All cleaned and everything. But who brought them? There's not a sign of a name."

"Hermit Dan," said Grandpa. "That's his way of doing things."

"Hermit Dan!" said the children.

"Is there a real hermit on the island?" asked Liza.

"He likes to think he is," said Grandpa. "His motto is you leave him alone and he'll leave you alone. You can sit by him fishing all afternoon and he may not say a single word."

"I've never known a real hermit," said Jed.

"Is he mean?" asked Bill.

"Do you call this mean?" asked Gran. "No, Dan helps the regular islanders in many ways. But he doesn't want you to mention it."

"But I understand he has a strong dislike for the summer people, especially the children. He tries to make them afraid of him so they won't come up his way," said Grandpa.

"Why?" said Jed. "Can't he just act the way he does with the islanders?"

"He could," said Grandpa. "But then he's afraid they would bother him. I hear his scaring tactics work pretty well. The summer people stay at their own end."

Gran had left them and dressed. She was already cooking the fish and making cornbread when they came in. Good smells came from the kitchen. The children went in and started setting the table.

"My," said Gran, "how you have grown up this year. You don't even need to be asked to do things."

"Tell Mom that, would you?" said Bill.

After supper Grandpa told the children more about the regular islanders and what to watch for. Soon they and their grandparents began to yawn.

"Does anybody need help in making beds?" asked Gran.

"We did that when we unpacked," said Liza. "Strict orders from Mom."

"Right now I'm just ready to get between those sheets," said Jed.

"So am I," said Bill. "I have a feeling tomorrow is going to be a day of adventures."

Everybody said their good-nights and went off to their rooms. Very shortly the waves pounding were the only sounds in the Roberts's house. Even Jelly Bean had curled up on the foot of Liza's bed and was fast asleep.

Liza's last thought before she dropped off was of a scraggly bush with red flowers.

9

The Early Bird

When Bill woke up the next morning, he went into the bathroom he shared with Jed. He whistled and sang while he washed and brushed his teeth. Finally Jed yelled, "Okay, that's enough. I'm awake."

Bill stuck his head in the door. He said, "Oh, I'm sorry. Did I wake you?"

"You know darn well you did," said Jed. "Now get out of the bathroom so I can use it."

Bill went back to his room and quickly dressed. Then he looked into Liza's room. She, too, was fast asleep. Bill pretended to stumble and almost fell into her room.

"What is it? What is it?" asked Liza.

"Oh," said Bill. "Sorry to wake you. I stumbled."

"Stumbled, my eye," said Jed, sticking his head out of the bathroom. "He just couldn't stand it because he was awake and we weren't. I suppose you'll wake Gran and Grandpa next."

"Oh, no," said Bill. "I would never do that. Besides, they're already awake. I checked."

Bill made such a funny face the other two couldn't help but laugh. Then he said, "Remember, this is a day for adventure."

"What kind of adventure?" asked Jed.

"To find a scraggly bush with red flowers," said Bill.

"That's right!" said Liza. "I almost forgot."

"Okay," said Jed. "You're forgiven."

He went back into his room to dress. Liza hurried to the bathroom. Bill headed for the kitchen. Gran and Grandpa were just coming in in wet swimsuits.

"Swimming this early!" said Bill.

"The best time," said Grandpa. "Gives you an appetite."

"Then remind me not to," said Bill. "I'm starving anyway."

"Get your cereal," said Gran. "I'll be down in a jiffy to make the rest of breakfast."

Gran and Grandpa went to their room. Bill got out the milk and cereal. Pretty soon Liza and Jed straggled into the kitchen.

Over breakfast the children asked more questions about the island. But their thoughts centered on that picture that was in Liza's room, the scraggly bush with red flowers.

There weren't many dishes to do. So the children were soon free.

Jed had one last question. He said, "Grandpa, do you remember which side of the back yard that bush was on?"

"What bush?" asked Grandpa.

"The one with the red flowers," said Jed.

Grandpa scratched his head and closed his eyes. Then he said, "That's been a lot of years ago. But I believe it was on the edge of the woods back of the right corner of the house." He nodded. "Yes, I'm sure that's where it was. But don't count on it still being there. Anything could have happened to it by now."

"We'll keep our fingers crossed," said Bill. "Is it all right if we go exploring?"

"Sure," said Gran. "There's nothing around here to hurt you. You could stay out all night and I don't think I would worry."

"Gee, thanks, Gran," said Jed. "This sure is different from home."

"Let's go, gang," said Bill.

"Wait a minute," said Jed. "Let's go to your room first, Liza."

"Whatever for?" asked Liza.

"You'll see," said Jed. He led the way. Jed walked straight to the picture. He stood looking at it.

"What are you looking for?" asked Bill. "It's just a picture. It's what I call a crummy first clue."

"Yes," said Jed. "But Grandpa said his brother was good at drawing. There are an awful lot of bushes back there. I want to get a picture of the shape of the leaf in my mind."

"Sometimes you do have brains," said Bill. "Come on, Liza, we'd better study that picture, too."

"But won't there be flowers?" asked Liza.

"Not necessarily," said Jed. "Different flowers and bushes bloom at different times."

"Should we take the picture with us?" asked Bill.

"No," said Jed. "Crummy or not, it's the only clue we have. We'd better leave it where it's safe."

"All right," said Liza. "I'm ready. Are you?"

"Right with you," said Bill.

The three children ran out to the back yard.

"Grandpa said the right side of the house," said Jed. "Boy, look at all those bushes."

"It's hopeless," said Liza. "Let's go swimming. We'll never find that bush."

"We won't if we don't look," said Jed.

"And it may not be there anymore," said Bill. "Let's not even try this mystery."

The three children looked at each other. Then they shook their heads.

"Nope," said Liza. "I think Grandpa is counting on us. We can't let him down. At least we've got to try."

"But shouldn't we have a plan or something?" asked Bill.

"Now you're talking," said Jed. "Let's divide the space."

This was soon done. The children began to look at every bush with leaves. No luck.

"Some bushes don't have their leaves yet," said Liza.

"You're right," said Jed. "I think we'd better find out more about this bush. Let's ask Grandpa what the name of it is."

"What good would that do?" asked Bill.

"Then we could look it up in the encyclopedia," said Jed. "Maybe that would tell us more about it."

"I think Grandpa could tell us more," said Liza.

"Yeah," said Bill. "School is out. Let's ask Grandpa."

"But we should do it so that he doesn't kno..
we're already having trouble. He'll be suspicious
if we just dash up to him."

"Liza is good at finding out things from him,"
said Bill. "Let's let her find out."

"Okay," said Liza. "I'll do my best. I just hope
Grandpa hasn't gone exploring himself. Where
will you be?"

"At the inlet," said Bill. "I'm ready for a swim.
And if that bush is there it can wait for another
hour or so."

"See you later, then," said Liza. She went to
find Grandpa. The boys went to put on their
swimsuits.

10

The Scraggly Bush

Liza went first to the kitchen. Gran was making out a list.

"What are you doing?" asked Liza.

"Making out my shopping list," said Gran. "The market boat comes tomorrow. I want to phone my order in today."

"Do you know where Grandpa is?" asked Liza.

"Yes," said Gran. "He's out in the tool shed."

"Thanks, Gran," said Liza. She started to go back outside. Then she changed her mind. She went to her room and put on her swimsuit. Then she went to the tool shed. Grandpa had fishing gear spread all over the work table.

"What are you doing?" asked Liza.

"Trying to get a little order in my things," said Grandpa. "I'm going to my favorite fishing spot. But I need special flies, and I have everything in a mess."

"Can I help?" asked Liza.

"No, thank you," said Grandpa. "I'm afraid I'll have to sort this out myself."

"I was hoping you'd go for a swim," said Liza.

"Not now," said Grandpa. "Remember, I swam before breakfast."

"That's right," said Liza. "I forgot. Grandpa, I want to ask you a question. I'm curious about something."

"Go right ahead," said Grandpa. "What are you curious about?"

"That bush," said Liza.

"What about the bush?" asked Grandpa.

"Well, you said it was never in bloom when you and Gran came," said Liza. "Just when does it bloom? Lots of other things are already blooming."

Grandpa thought a minute. Then he said. "I think it should start almost anytime now. It's a queer bush."

"What's queer about it?" asked Liza.

"The flowers come out before the leaves," said Grandpa. "I know other bushes do that, too, but this one looks queer. The bush is scraggly and then come those bright red flowers and no leaves."

Liza laughed. She said, "I want to see that. Are there any other bushes like that around here?"

"I can't rightly say," said Grandpa. "I've never seen one. My mother brought that one to the island."

"Does it grow big?" asked Liza.

"No," said Grandpa. "That's another odd thing about it. It grows about three feet high. Then after its season it dies down. The next season there's new growth. But I've never seen it get over about three feet high."

"Does it have a name?" asked Liza.

"I'm sure it does," said Grandpa. "But I don't know what it is."

Suddenly Grandpa spotted the fly he had been

looking for. He exclaimed, "There it is! Now I can go fishing."

"And I'll catch up with the boys," said Liza. "Good luck fishing."

"Thanks, dear," said Grandpa. "Have a good swim."

Liza ran in the direction of the inlet. She could hear the boys shouting and splashing. Soon she was making as much noise as they were.

"I'm sure glad this inlet isn't close to anybody else's house," said Jed. "They might complain about the noise."

"I asked Grandpa about it," said Bill. "He said the beach was on our property. So it's our own private swimming pool."

"And it's the best I've ever seen," said Liza. "Just think, we can go swimming whenever we want."

"Say, Liza," said Jed. "Did you find out anything from Grandpa?"

"Did I ever!" said Liza.

"So come on. Tell us," said Bill.

Since the children had no towels they started back toward the house. Liza told the boys what she had found out.

"Good girl!" said Jed. "That gives us a lot more to go on."

"Let's dress and start looking now," said Bill. "I think we might even be successful."

In just a few minutes the children were dressed and in the back yard. Gran called, "I'm going over to the Widow Hawkins. I want her recipe for that cake she made us."

"We want you to have it," said Bill. "That cake was scrumptious."

"Now the coast is really clear," said Jed. "How shall we go about this?"

"Just as we planned. We each know our section," said Liza. "We shouldn't miss any."

"That's a good idea," said Bill.

Then Jed stopped. He said, "I think I want to look at that picture again."

"But we went all through that," said Bill.

"I know," said Jed. "But this time I want to look at the shape."

"I know what you mean," said Liza. "We have to imagine the shape of the bush with no leaves and no flowers."

"It sounds crazy to me," said Bill. "But let's take a look."

The children were in and out of the house in a few minutes.

"Okay," said Bill.. "Get started. I feel as if I should have a magnifying glass."

The other two were too busy to answer. They looked at each bush carefully. But not one was like the scraggly one in the picture. Bill finished first. He sat down and waited for the others. Finally they joined him.

"I think this is one mystery we won't solve," said Bill.

"It's going to be a tough one," said Jed. "But I'm not ready to give up yet. What about you, Liza?"

"Me! Give up?" said Liza. "Of course not. We just started."

"But that picture is the only clue," said Bill. "And we got nowhere with it. Do you think Grandpa had the sides of the house wrong?"

"No," said Jed. "He would have remembered. The tool shed and those other buildings are on the other side."

"I know," said Bill. "We can just wait until the bush starts blooming. That will make things easy."

"We may have to do that," said Jed.

Suddenly Liza spotted something. It was a bush in Bill's section. She knelt down beside it.

"Yippee," she shouted. Both boys ran to her. They said, "What is it? What is it?"

Then Jed saw. He said, "Hey, this bush is in bud."

"Yes," said Liza, "and see the little tip of red? It looks like the right shape to me, too."

"It sure does," said Jed. He turned to Bill and said, "I think you could have used that magnifying glass after all."

"Yep," said Bill. "I'm sure glad you two are around. Shall we tell Gran and Grandpa now?"

"Are you kidding?" said Liza and Jed.

"Grandpa gave us this mystery to solve. We'll tell him when we solve it," said Jed.

"And not before," said Liza.

"So what's the next step?" asked Bill.

"Well, the next clue isn't on the bush so it must be under the bush," said Jed.

"That means we dig," said Bill. "I should have known."

"Let's see what's in the tool shed to dig with," said Liza.

11

The Bush's Clue

On the way to the tool shed, the children met Grandpa.

"What's your rush?" asked Grandpa. "Don't you want to see what I've got?"

The children stopped. Grandpa proudly held up a string of five fish. He said, "See, I caught just what we needed. That's why there are always fish there. The islanders take just what they need."

"They're beauties," said Jed. "Will you take us with you one day?"

"Nope," said Grandpa. "You'll have to find this place yourself."

"But, Grandpa," said Liza. "What about the summer people? Are they as careful as the islanders?"

"I doubt if they would be," said Grandpa. "But this is private property. They aren't allowed up here. And so far there's been no trouble. Hermit Dan makes sure of that. But you three will find the place soon. You're real snoopers."

"Are you going to take them in to Gran?" asked Bill. He was in a hurry to get to the tool shed.

"Not until they're dressed," said Grandpa. "Gran is not at all interested in fish with scales on them. Come along. I'll teach you how to dress fish. I'll just get some more knives."

"But Grandpa, we need—" started Bill. But Jed nudged him hard. Bill turned red.

"You need what?" asked Grandpa.

"It's not important," said Bill.

"Come on, Grandpa," said Liza. "Let's get the knives and get these fish dressed."

It was the last thing the children wanted to do. But they knew the quicker they did it, the quicker they would be free again.

Grandpa laid fresh paper on a wooden table. He showed the children how to scale the fish. Then he gave each of them a fish and a knife. After they scaled them to suit Grandpa, he showed them how to open them.

"Ugh," said Jed. "They smell. I'm like Gran. I don't want to see another fish with scales on it."

Grandpa laughed and went right on with his lesson. Soon the fish were done. The children were free. They ran to the outdoor pump to wash their hands.

"They still smell," said Jed. "I'm going inside and use soap."

"Ahh," said Bill. "Who minds a little fishy smell?"

"I do," said Liza. "I'm going in, too. You can get the tools, Bill."

"Oh, well, I'll go in, too," said Bill. "Come to think of it, fish is not my favorite perfume."

Soon the children were back at the tool shed.

"Hey, we're lucky," said Bill. "Here are two spades. We can take turns."

"Did anybody ask if it was all right to dig?" asked Liza.

"Who cares?" asked Bill. "We'll cover the holes back up."

"I think Bill is right, Liza," said Jed. "If we ask about digging, Grandpa will know we're up to something. But if we dig and cover the holes, it won't hurt anything."

"Then let's get started," said Liza.

"Just a minute," said Jed. "Say, Liza, didn't that picture have some straight marks on it?"

"Yes," said Liza. "Shall I get the picture?"

"Please," said Jed. "Maybe it will make things simpler."

Liza was back with the picture in a minute.

"Did you see Gran and Grandpa?" asked Bill.

"Grandpa was headed over toward the Widow Hawkins's house," said Liza. "I guess Gran is still there."

"Good," said Jed. "Let me see the picture."

"Yep," he said. "I thought so. See those dashes? I think they mean something."

All three children studied the picture. They couldn't figure it out.

"Maybe it means steps from the bush," said Bill.

"That's what I think, too," said Liza.

"You're probably right," said Jed. "But in what direction?"

"This way," said Bill and Liza. They each pointed in a different direction. Jed laughed.

"That's what I mean," he said. "It would depend on where Grandpa's brother was standing when he made the picture."

"Boy, no mystery is easy," said Bill. "That means we have to dig in four directions."

"Are you sure there wasn't another spade in that shed?" asked Liza.

"No, but there was a hoe if you want that," said Jed.

Liza ran to the shed. She came back shouting, "I found something better." She held up a trowel and said, "I can dig better with this than a spade."

"Good for you," said Jed. "Now let's figure out where each of us should dig."

They looked at the picture again. They counted the dashes.

"Okay," said Bill. "We know it's ten steps. Of course we don't know what size steps."

"And we know it goes straight out from the

bush," said Liza. "And Great-Uncle John was the oldest so his feet were probably bigger than ours. Bill, you have the biggest feet. You count it out."

"Good idea, Liza," said Jed. "Go ahead, Bill. Take biggish steps. Then we can get some idea as to where to dig."

"I knew my big feet would come in handy some day," said Bill. He started counting out the steps in four directions. Jed marked the places Bill stopped with a stone.

"Okay, gang," said Bill. "Start digging."

"I wish I knew what we were digging for," said Liza.

"It would help," said Jed. "But we don't. Just be careful to look through all the dirt you dig."

"And dig in a big circle because Grandpa's brother may have taken bigger steps than Bill," said Liza.

The children worked in silence for quite a while. They would dig a spadeful of soil. Then they would sift it through their hands. But it was just soil.

Finally Bill's shovel clunked against something.

"Hey," he called. "I hit something different."

He was on his knees digging with his hands the

same way Jelly Bean dug. In fact Jelly Bean came along. He sniffed at the hole. But it didn't smell interesting so he left.

"I got it! I got it!" said Bill.

"What is it?" said Liza and Jed.

"It's a jar and there's something in it," said Bill. "But I can't get the top off."

"Here, let me have it," said Jed. "You all stand back."

Liza and Bill moved back. Jed picked up a stone

and dropped it on the jar. The jar shattered. He said, "Okay, I'll get it out. We'd better remember to pick up all this broken glass though."

Jed pulled out a paper. It was rolled up. Carefully he unrolled it. Bill and Liza looked over his shoulder.

"Oh, no! Another picture," said Bill. "This is harder than codes."

"It is a code," said Liza, "a picture code."

"Well, if I ever hide a treasure I'm going to just say what you're supposed to do."

"But that would be no fun," said Jed. "What is it?"

"It's a picture of a nut tree," said Liza. "It looks like our hickory-nut tree."

"But how does that help us?" said Bill. "There must be a lot of nut trees around here."

"We'll take it in and study it," said Jed. "I'm afraid Gran and Grandpa will be back soon. Remember, we said we would fill in the holes."

"Yes," said Liza. "And do be careful about the glass."

Soon the holes were filled in and the glass buried. Bill said, "There, that's done. Let's go."

"Uh-uh," said Jed. "Not good enough. We've

got to scatter some stuff over the ground. Anybody can see where we were digging."

"I wish you weren't so smart sometimes," said Bill. But he began to cover the traces of their digging. Then they put the tools away and went inside to study the picture.

12

The Scary Night

Just as the children got inside, Gran and Grandpa arrived, too. Quickly Jed slipped the picture into his pocket.

"Good," said Gran. "I'm glad you're here. Grandpa and I need your help."

"Yes," said Grandpa. "Gran and I would like to rearrange things a bit. You know, get them so we will feel at home. Will you help us?"

"Sure thing," said Bill. "Just tell us what to do."

Jelly Bean was yapping at the door. He wanted in.

"I suppose first things first," said Gran. "Liza, do see what's wrong with that puppy. I imagine he's hungry. The way he races about! He really loves it here."

Jed took a minute or two to slip into Liza's room. He put the picture in a safe place. When he came back he nodded to the other two children. They knew what he meant. Now all they hoped was that there wasn't too much work to do. That picture was all they could think of.

But Gran and Grandpa kept them busy for hours moving furniture. Finally Grandpa said, "That's enough for today. By my watch it's getting on to supper time. And tonight, I'm going to cook."

"You, Grandpa?" said Bill.

"Yes, me," said Grandpa. "And I don't need any help. Out, out, all of you."

Gran laughed. She said, "Don't mind him. He gets this way every so often. Put on your swimsuits and we'll have a lesson."

The children were glad enough to do that. It was good to relax in the water after all that work.

Later Gran said, "I expect your grandfather is ready for us now. Let's go home and eat."

"I'm glad you said that," said Bill. "I'm starved."

"I'm a bit hungry myself," said Gran.

"Come on," said Bill. "Let's race to the house."

"You boys go ahead," said Liza. "I want to walk with Gran."

"I'm with you," said Jed. "Let's run."

The two boys took off. By the time Gran and Liza got home they were dressed and setting the table.

"Hmm," said Liza. "That smells good."

Grandpa smiled, "It should. It's fish cooked by my secret recipe. Not even Gran knows it."

Later, after they had eaten and the dishes had been done, they sat on the front porch. There were rocking chairs and a swing there. The easy motion made the tired children begin to yawn.

Gran looked at them. She said, "You've had quite a day. So off to bed with you. Tomorrow will come very soon."

For once the children didn't argue. Soon they were in bed. Nobody had trouble getting to sleep that night.

But the children were awakened before long. They heard Jelly Bean yapping. Then Gran and

Grandpa were shouting. "Corner him! Corner him! Then maybe we can get him out."

The children were terrified. Bill yelled, "What's happening?"

They all ran into the hall. Jed said, "What do you suppose it is?"

"It's a burglar, I'll bet," said Bill. "Gran probably has the poker and Grandpa has his gun."

"No," said Liza. "They keep shouting to corner him. They wouldn't corner a burglar. He might have a gun, too."

"Well, whatever it is," said Jed, "it sounds awful."

"Shouldn't we hide or lock the door or something?" said Liza.

"Are you completely nuts?" asked Bill. "We're going down and help Gran and Grandpa."

The children put on their slippers and hurried downstairs. What a strange sight they saw! Jelly Bean was hopping up and down and yapping as loud as he could. Gran was flapping a newspaper and Grandpa was running around the room with a broom.

"What is it? What is it?" asked Liza.

"A bat," said Gran. "And I can't stand the things."

"We're trying to corner him so we can put him outside," said Grandpa.

"Need some help?" asked Jed.

"Yes," said Gran. "Get some more newspaper and help me scare him into a corner.

Liza reached for her hair. She said, "But I heard bats were dangerous. If they get in your hair they won't turn loose. I don't want to have a bat cut out of my hair. I don't want short hair."

Everybody laughed. Grandpa said, "Nothing to that story."

The laughing made Liza mad. She said, "All right! I'll get that bat. And if I have to have my hair cut off it will be your fault."

Liza waved her newspaper around. She hopped on chairs and tables. Finally the poor bat gave up. It just hit the floor and stayed there.

"See," said Liza, "I told you I would get him."

"All right, all right," said Bill.

"I just hope you didn't ruin any furniture," said Gran. "Thank you boys for staying on the floor."

Gran started to say more, but they heard Grandpa say, "Now would you look at that!"

They all went over to where Grandpa was kneeling beside the bat.

"Look at what?" asked Gran.

"That plucky little thing," said Grandpa. "We were scaring her to death and her carrying all that extra weight."

They all looked down. Clutched to the bat was a baby bat.

Liza dropped to her knees beside the bat. She said, "I'm sorry. We didn't know. We weren't going to hurt you. Grandpa just wanted to put you outside where you belong."

The bat was too terrified to move. Liza flung her arms around Gran.

"Oh, Gran! Grandpa, please put her outside in a safe place. I'll never be scared of bats again."

Grandpa took a dustpan. Carefully he put the mother and her baby on the pan. Then he took them out back and put them in a safe place.

Things were quiet when he got back. The children were filled with questions. Jed said, "How did she get in, Grandpa? There are screens on the windows."

"Probably came in through the chimney. Bats often sleep in chimneys because they like the dark. They hunt food at night."

"Was that the kind of bat that sucks blood?" asked Bill.

"That bat?" said Gran. "You saw it. It wouldn't hurt anything. We wanted it out for its own sake. You're thinking of vampire bats. We have none of those around here."

Suddenly Liza said, "I'm freezing."

"It has gotten chilly," said Gran. "I'm going to make a pot of hot chocolate. It will help us all to get to sleep."

"It has been a rather exciting night," said Grandpa. "I think I'll light a little fire."

"Oh, no!" said Liza. "Please don't, Grandpa. You might burn the bat's nest."

"But bats don't have nests," said Grandpa. "No bats are in the chimney now. They're all out hunting food."

"But what about their eggs?" said Bill. "With no nests, where do they lay them?"

"Bat's don't lay eggs," said Grandpa.

"But I thought all birds laid eggs," said Jed.

"Bats aren't birds," said Grandpa.

"They aren't?" said Bill.

"Didn't you look closely at that bat?" said Grandpa.

"Yes," said Liza.

"Did you see any feathers?" asked Grandpa.

"Come to think of it, no," said Jed. "It had fur. In fact it looked like a mouse with wings. But the wings weren't like a bird's."

"That's right," said Grandpa, "Bats belong to the same class of animals as you do. They are the only flying mammals."

"But what about their babies?" asked Liza. "How does a mother get one?"

"The same way your mother did. The baby bats grow inside their mothers," said Grandpa.

Just then Gran stuck her head in the door. She said, "A fire! Good. Someone help me bring in the hot chocolate. And no more bat talk. Your grandfather gave me the same lecture when we ran into our first bat."

The children laughed and went to help Gran. The hot chocolate and warm fire made everybody drowsy. Even Jelly Bean curled up and went to sleep. Soon everybody was ready to go back to bed.

13

The Heart Tree

The children were all in good moods the next morning. Sleep had made the scary night seem far away. After breakfast they went into Liza's room.

"Now get the picture," said Bill. "Let's see what's next."

"I don't know where it is," said Liza. "Jed put it away."

"So I did," said Jed. "Here it is under this book.

I didn't want Gran or Grandpa to see it."

"Aren't we going to tell them anything?" said Bill.

"Sure we are," said Liza.

"When we find the treasure," said Jed.

Liza got the picture.

"It still just looks like a hickory-nut tree to me," said Bill.

"But it must mean something," said Jed. "We thought the other picture was just a scraggly bush, but those dashes were the clue to that code."

"Well, there aren't any dashes on this," said Liza.

"But there's a hole in the tree," said Bill. "Maybe that means something."

"Oh, pooh," said Liza. "Lots of trees have holes in them."

Jed was silent through all of this. Suddenly he said, "Does anybody have a magnifying glass?"

"A magnifying glass!" said Liza and Bill. "What for?"

"I think there's something funny about the trunk of the tree," said Jed. "But I can't quite make it out. Gosh, I wish I had brought my magnifying glass."

"Gran has a big one," said Liza. "Remember how Grandpa teases her?"

"Yeah," said Bill. "And she just says as long as they make the print smaller she has to make it larger with her magnifying glass."

"Think she'll let us borrrow it?" asked Jed.

"Oh, sure," said Liza. "You know Gran. I'll go and ask her."

Liza ran to the kitchen. Grandpa was having another cup of coffee and talking to Gran.

"And what are you up to?" he said when Liza came in.

"We want to borrow Gran's magnifying glass," said Liza.

"Magnifying glass," said Grandpa. "Now why do you need a magnifying glass?"

"We just wanted to make something big," said Liza. She winked at Gran.

Gran laughed and said, "Go ahead and take it. It's in the desk drawer. Just be sure to put it back. You know how I like to make things big, too."

"Thanks, Gran," said Liza. She ran to get the magnifying glass. She took it to the boys.

"Success," she said. She handed it to Jed. Jed immediately began to search the picture for clues. Suddenly he shouted, "That's it!"

"What's it?" asked Bill.

"Take a look at the trunk of the tree," he said. He handed the magnifying glass to Bill. Bill looked at the trunk of the tree.

"Gee," he said. "You're right. It has letters on it."

"Do hurry," said Liza. "I want to see, too."

Bill handed the magnifying glass to her. Liza looked and grinned.

"What's funny?" said Jed.

"The heart," said Liza.

"What heart?" asked Bill and Jed.

"Take a look," said Liza.

"She's right," said Jed. "There is a heart there."

He gave the glass to Bill. Bill looked and said, "Why, so there is! Now I suppose all the trees in the woods have to be checked for hearts."

"Oh, cut it out, Bill," said Jed. "I expect Grandpa will remember all about it."

"But you said we weren't going to tell," said Bill.

"We aren't," said Jed. "You know how easy it is to get Grandpa to tell a story."

"We'll go swimming and ask him to come along," said Liza. "He likes to sit in the sun."

"Good idea," said Bill. "I'm ready for a swim."

The children put on their swimsuits. Liza remembered to return the magnifying glass.

"We're going swimming," said Jed to Gran and Grandpa. "Come with us."

"We'll be down a little later," said Grandpa. "Gran wants to finish something here first."

"We'll see you at the beach," said Liza.

"Grandpa doesn't like to stay in the water long," said Bill. "We'll get out when he does."

"We'd better do it one at a time so he won't think we're up to something," said Liza.

"Atta girl," said Bill. "You do have brains after all."

"I wish I could say the same for you," said Liza.

"I might surprise you one day," said Bill.

"It would be a surprise all right," said Liza.

Grandpa was as good as his word. A little later he came down. And Bill was right. After swimming for a bit, he got out of the water. He put a towel on the sand and stretched out in the sun. Liza waited a while. Then she went and sat by him.

"Grandpa," she said, "are there any fruit trees besides plums on the island?"

"Oh, yes," said Grandpa. "There are loads of

them. My father planted a lot of them. And Hermit Dan plants more each year, they tell me."

"What do they do with all the fruit?" asked Liza.

"Eat a lot of it, sell some to the summer people, and can or freeze the rest for the off season. Hermit Dan has a deal with the Widow Hawkins. He gathers the fruit and she cans it."

"That's a pretty good deal," said Liza. "What about nuts? Are there any nut trees around?"

"Yes, there are several kinds," said Grandpa. Then he started laughing.

Liza looked puzzled.

"Sorry," said Grandpa. "That just made me remember something."

"Oh, do tell me," said Liza.

"All right," said Grandpa. "When we were children we had a favorite tree."

"We have two of them," said Liza, "one at your house and one at ours."

"I know," said Grandpa. "But this was a nut tree. We called it our 'initial' tree."

"Initial tree," said Liza. "Why?"

"Because we had all cut our initials on it," said Grandpa.

"What kind of a nut tree was it?" asked Liza.

Gran walked up just then. She said, "It was a hickory-nut tree."

"Did you carve your initials on it, too?" asked Liza. She was so excited she could hardly sit still.

"I didn't, but your grandfather's brother did," said Gran. "Your Great-Aunt Mary was my best friend when we were children. So the family invited me to spend the summer with them on the island. Your Great-Uncle John liked to tease me. So one day he carved a heart and put your grandfather's and my initials in it. Then he told me he had something to show me. He took me to the tree. There was that freshly carved heart.

Grandpa roared with laughter. He said, "Gran was so embarrassed she wouldn't even come down for supper. Of course we never dreamed at that time that some day we would be married."

Liza looked at Gran and began giggling. She said, "Gran, you're blushing."

The boys heard the laughter and came running.

"What is it? What is it?" said Jed.

"Yeah, let us in on it," said Bill.

"Your grandfather will tell you the story," said Gran. "I'm going for a swim."

A little later the children left. But not before

they had found out where the initial tree was. The boys patted Liza on the back.

"Good going," they said.

Liza began to giggle again. She couldn't get over Gran. After all these years still blushing over something that had happened to a little girl.

14

Delayed Plans

As they walked home Bill said, "Now at least we know where the tree is."

"But we don't know what to look for," said Liza. "Our Great-Uncle John was a tricky one."

"You know I'm named after him," said Jed.

"How do you get Jed out of John?" asked Bill.

"You don't," said Jed. "But that's what I called myself when I was a baby. So that's what everybody called me."

"Had a hard time talking, huh?" said Bill.

"But at least I could think," said Jed.

"Well, start thinking now," said Liza. "What do we do next?"

Jed didn't say anything. But Bill and Liza knew he was thinking. So they were quiet. Jed was the best thinker of the three.

Finally he said, "We missed something on that picture. We'd better go back to the house and borrow Gran's magnifying glass again. Our uncle really hid this clue."

The children changed from their swimsuits. They put the suits out to dry. Then they went to Liza's room.

"Here, Jed," said Liza. "You take the magnifying glass. All I'll see is that heart. I still can't get over Gran."

"You get pretty embarrassed yourself when you get teased," said Bill. "Remember when we said Joey was your boy friend?"

"Embarrassed!" said Jed. "Liza doesn't get embarrassed. She just starts throwing things. You got clonked on the head that time."

"Yeah," said Bill. "I got a real knot out of that."

"Okay," said Liza. "Be serious. It will soon be

lunch time. Let's be ready to go after that."

Jed studied the picture. He said, "I just can't find it. But Great-Uncle John sure could draw."

"Here," said Bill. "Let me take a look."

Bill studied the picture for a few minutes. Then he said, "Uh-huh, just as I thought."

"What do you mean?" said Liza.

"I said the tree had a hole in it when I first saw the picture," said Bill.

"So?" said Liza.

"You just said lots of trees have holes in them," said Bill. "Take a close look at this one."

"Look, Jed!" she cried. "Bill is right."

Jed took the picture. He said, "By gosh, that's it! How did I miss that little 'x' mark in the middle of the hole?"

"Because you were trying to make an easy thing hard," said Bill.

"Oh, oh," said Liza. "Here we go again. Every time he does something special he has to brag."

"Well, let him this time," said Jed. "I sure didn't see that clue."

"You see, I do have brains," said Bill. Then he added, "Sometimes."

Liza and Jed had to laugh at the funny face he made.

"I hear Gran and Grandpa coming back," said Jed. "Don't give anything away."

"Trust us, trust us," said Bill.

"Let's go and help with lunch," said Liza. "That way we can get away quicker."

"And eat sooner," said Bill.

"He never changes," said Jed. "It's food, food, food. And yet he never gets fat."

"I'm a growing boy," said Bill, and ran down the stairs.

"We came to help with lunch," said Liza.

"I won't need any help today," said Gran.

"No," said Grandpa. "We're invited out. Didn't Gran tell you?"

"No," said Liza.

"Oh, dear," said Gran. "I thought I had. Anyway, the Widow Hawkins has fixed a special lunch for us."

Liza started to say something, but Bill punched her. He said, "That's fine."

"Do we have to dress up?" asked Jed.

"Good heavens, no," said Gran. "But we do have to get out of these wet swimsuits. You three just brush your hair a little."

"You never have to dress up on the island," said Grandpa.

Gran and Grandpa went to their room.

"Wouldn't you know it?" said Liza. "Today of all days."

"Oh, cheer up," said Jed. "It's just for lunch. We had to eat anyway. We'll still have time to go to the tree."

"And besides that," said Bill, "the Widow Hawkins sure can cook."

"Yes," said Jed, "and no dishes to wash."

"You want to bet?" said Liza.

"What do you mean?" asked Bill.

"Well, you know we have to offer to help," said Liza.

"But I'll bet the Widow Hawkins won't let us," said Jed, "I'll bet she doesn't want anybody in her kitchen."

"I hope you're right," said Liza. "Let's go and brush our hair."

They were soon on their way.

"I see other houses, but no people," said Bill. "Are they inside eating?"

"They could be," said Grandpa. "Or they could be at the other end of the island making sure the houses are ready for the summer people. That's how the islanders pick up extra money. They check on the resort houses to make sure everything is all right and dusted before the owners come."

"Oh," said Jed. "Is that where Hermit Dan is?"

"Good gracious, no!" said Grandpa. "Dan wouldn't touch the summer people with a ten-foot pole."

"Where does he live?"

"Just along the way. You can see it from here. It's that little hut."

"But it's so small," said Liza.

"There used to be a fine frame house there. But it burned down. Then Dan put up that hut. He said it was enough room for him."

"How does he make a living?" asked Bill.

"It doesn't take much to live here," said Grandpa. "I think he has a little pension. And he grows or hunts most of his food."

"I don't see any garden," said Jed.

"His garden is on our land," said Grandpa.

"Our land!" said Liza.

"You see," said Gran "that's another nice thing about the island. It's just like one big family. When there was nobody to take over the garden plot the Roberts family had cleared, Dan did it. He probably supplies most of the islanders with vegetables."

"He has a flock of chickens and a cow back there in the woods, too," said Grandpa.

"Yes," said Gran. "Just this morning, I found a dozen fresh eggs at the back door."

"And he hates it if you thank him," said Grandpa. "He scowls if you even smile at him."

"He sounds like a real oddball to me," said Bill.

"He's fine as long as you let him be," said Gran.

"Hey, Mrs. Hawkins!" cried Grandpa. "We're coming, and we're mighty hungry."

Mrs. Hawkins leaned out of the window and called, "Come on then. Everything is ready."

15

Jelly Bean Trouble

Everybody stuffed themselves on the good food. Even Jelly Bean was given a dish of scraps. But the big surprise was the dessert.

"Strawberry shortcake!" said Bill. His eyes got big. "Wow!" he said.

"Yes," said Mrs. Hawkins. "Dan brought the berries over. They are the first of his second crop. He says it's going to be a good one. So I expect I'll be making jam soon."

"This whipped cream is the best I ever tasted," said Liza.

"That's thanks to Dan, too," said Mrs. Hawkins. "He really keeps me supplied with food."

"He sounds like an interesting man," said Jed. "I'd like to meet him."

"You would be better off to keep at a distance," said Mrs. Hawkins.

"Why?" asked Liza.

"Dan is a fine person," said Mrs. Hawkins. "He's a friend to all the islanders. He doesn't talk much. He just does nice things. But for some reason he can't stand children."

"Why not?" asked Jed.

"Nobody knows," said Mrs. Hawkins. "It's been true as long as I've known him. So just take a tip and stay out of his way."

"Gee, I'm sorry to hear that," said Liza. "I was looking forward to meeting him."

"You probably will," said Mrs. Hawkins.

Gran and Grandpa added a few bits of information about Hermit Dan. Then Mrs. Hawkins said, "Now, I know you children want to get out. So run along and have fun."

"Don't you want us to do the dishes?" asked Liza.

"Bless you, child," said Mrs. Hawkins. "But I'm rather set in my ways. I'd rather do the cleaning myself."

"Well, thank you for lunch," said Jed.

"Yes," said Bill. "It was scrumptious."

Then Bill walked over to Mrs. Hawkins and hugged her. He said, "You're a nice woman."

The children left.

"Now," said Jed, "let's get on our way."

"Yes," said Liza. "Initial tree, here we come. Do you think we need the picture?"

"No," said Bill. "But we do need to walk slowly. I'm so stuffed. The food has to have a chance to settle down a little."

"Bill's right," said Jed. "I ate too much myself. That woman sure can cook."

"Oh, look. Jelly Bean decided to come, too," said Liza.

"Do you remember last summer when Jelly Bean got trapped?" asked Bill.

"Who could forget?" said Jed. "We thought he was dead. But he was trapped in one of the clues in the woods."

"That would never happen now," said Bill. "He has a loud yap for a small dog."

"Well, come on," said Liza, "or we'll never get to the tree today."

The children walked through the woods. Suddenly they heard a loud yapping.

"Oh, oh, that's Jelly Bean," said Jed. "He's wandered off."

"He's probably chasing a squirrel," said Bill. "He'll catch up with us."

But Liza was not sure. She said, "I think we'd better take a look."

"Oh, all right," said Bill. They started toward the yapping. And what they saw made them all stop in their tracks.

"Oh, no!" said Liza. She covered her eyes. Jelly Bean was face-to-face with a skunk. The skunk growled at Jelly Bean. Jelly Bean yapped at the skunk.

"Jelly Bean!" shouted Jed, "come back."

But Jelly Bean paid no attention. He went on yapping. The skunk began to stamp his feet.

"Please, Jelly Bean," said Liza. "Please come back."

Still Jelly Bean paid no attention.

"Throw a stick at him," said Bill. "Maybe that will make him move."

"No, don't," said Jed. "We might hit the skunk. Then Jelly Bean would be in trouble for sure."

"He's going to be in it for sure anyway," said Bill.

"Jelly Bean! Please, Jelly Bean, come back," cried Liza.

Jelly Bean gave another yap. Then he turned just as the skunk turned. He started toward the children. But he didn't get out of the way fast enough. His whole backside was sprayed by the skunk. Jelly Bean gave a yap of surprise at the horrible smell.

"Now what do we do?" asked Bill.

"Let's get him to the stream," said Jed. "We aren't too far from the house. Bill, you're the fastest runner. Go get that soap Grandpa uses when he's been doing dirty work."

Liza picked up Jelly Bean and ran to the stream. The smell almost made her sick.

"Dump him in the water and I'll hold him," said Jed. Then he added, "You know, you'll smell like skunk, too."

"Why?" asked Liza. "The skunk didn't spray me."

"No, but you picked up Jelly Bean," said Jed. "It will be on you."

Jelly Bean didn't like the water, but Jed held him in it and rubbed his fur.

Soon Bill got back with the soap. "Here," he said. "I brought two kinds. Here's Grandpa's first. Then I brought Gran's lavender soap. I thought that might help."

"Good thinking," said Jed. "Here, I'll soap him."

Poor Jelly Bean. He had never had such a bath. But finally he stopped squirming and just let them wash him.

"Well, that's the best I can do," said Jed. He turned Jelly Bean loose. Jelly Bean ran in circles, shaking himself and rolling over and over.

"That helps some," said Bill. "But it sure smells bad around here. Let's get on. We can pick up the soap on the way back."

Suddenly Liza said, "I can't stand it."

"Now what?" asked Bill.

"It's me," said Liza. "I can't stand the smell of me. I think I'm going to be sick."

"Get in the stream," said Jed.

"With my clothes on?" asked Liza.

"Yes," said Jed. "They smell, too. Lie down so the water will go all over you. Hand her the soap, Bill."

Liza washed herself the best she could. But she was still unhappy. "It's awful. I'm so smelly."

"Come on," said Jed. "The initial tree will have to wait. We need help. I'm beginning to feel sick myself."

"Ruined plans," said Bill. He followed his brother, sister and dog home.

They got to the back door and started to go in. Gran came running out.

"Shoo," she said. "Don't bring that skunk smell into this house."

The children were surprised. They didn't know what to do.

"But we need help," said Jed. Liza started to cry.

"Just get back from the house," said Gran. "I'll help you. Let me get some warm water.

Grandpa came out then. Gran said, "These children have tangled with a skunk. Get some soap and towels."

"We've got soap," said Bill. He held up the two bars.

"My good lavender soap!" said Gran. "How could you?"

The children were surprised. Gran didn't often get angry with them.

"We're sorry, Gran," said Bill. "We thought it would help. We tried to stop Jelly Bean. But he just wouldn't come to us."

Grandpa just laughed. Everybody looked at him. He said, "You're the sorriest-looking crew I ever saw." He looked at the boys and said, "Just who got sprayed?"

"Jelly Bean got sprayed. Then Liza picked him up and took him to the stream. I washed him," said Jed.

"Then it's Liza and Jelly Bean who are carrying the smell. You boys come with me. You take a hot soapy shower and wash your hair. I'll take your clothes out and let them air. You'll be all right. Then I'll tend to Jelly Bean while Gran takes care of Liza."

The boys quickly went to their rooms and gave Grandpa their clothes. He stopped by Liza's room and got her robe. Then he went to help Gran.

"Oh, Gran," Liza was saying. "Please don't be angry. I'm sorry. I just didn't know what to do."

"My dear," said Gran. "I'm not angry at you. I'm just angry at the situation. But I do wish that foolish puppy had a little more sense."

"I expect he does, too, now," said Grandpa.

But it wasn't long before things were in order. Liza hardly smelled at all. Jelly Bean still smelled, but not as much as he had. Then the family could laugh at the day's problems. And the children turned their attention back to the initial tree.

16

What a Morning

Early the next morning Jed said, "Gran, we're going exploring in the woods, okay?"

"Certainly," said Gran. "Just stay away from that skunk."

"We were thinking about that," said Liza. "Could you keep Jelly Bean shut up until we get away?"

"You don't have to worry," said Gran. "Jelly Bean went off with Grandpa to the inlet. I'm going to join them."

"Good," said Bill. "We'll see you at lunch time."

The children started into the woods.

"Gee, it's a beautiful day," said Liza.

"Gran says every day is beautiful here," said Jed.

"But it has to rain sometime," said Bill.

"Yeah," said Jed. "But who minds rain when it's warm?"

Suddenly the children heard a thrashing of the bushes.

"Quick! Hide!" said Jed.

The children almost dived into the bushes. They huddled together. The thrashing came nearer. Then they heard a voice.

"You might as well come out. I know you're hiding somewhere in those bushes," said the voice. "And I've had enough of you. You don't belong on the island."

"Gosh," whispered Bill. "Do you think he means us?"

"He must. I haven't seen anybody else around."

"Shh," said Jed. "He's coming closer."

An old man came into sight. His hair was almost white. He had a gun over one shoulder and a stick in his other hand. He was walking rapidly and thrashing the bushes.

"Hermit Dan!" whispered the children.

"It just has to be," whispered Liza.

"You aren't going to get into my corn again. And I know it was you. You left your smell everywhere. You and that raccoon. I would like to kill you."

Closer and closer came Hermit Dan. The children were afraid to even whisper. But Hermit Dan went right on talking and passed them right by.

The children waited in the bushes until Hermit Dan was well past them.

"Boy," said Bill. "I see what Widow Hawkins means. I've seen all I want to of Hermit Dan."

"What was he so mad about?" asked Liza.

"Something got in his corn last night," said Jed.

"And I think the something was our skunk," said Bill. "I don't know of anything else that would leave a smell."

"Do skunks like corn?" asked Liza.

"I think they like all kinds of things," said Jed.

"Anyway, he didn't head toward the initial tree," said Bill. "Let's be on our way."

The children were quite shaken up. But they

were too excited about getting to the tree to turn back. Finally they saw it.

"It's a big one," said Bill.

Liza ran ahead. She called, "Here's the heart and all the other initials. It's like it was in the picture. Just think, Gran and Grandpa were children when the carvings were made."

The children looked at the tree. They were quite awed by it. Here before them was family history. And perhaps the tree would disclose even more.

Bill was the first to speak.

"Okay," he said, "where's the hole?"

"It's above the heart," said Jed. "Can't you see?"

"But in the picture it looked low," said Bill. "We can't reach that."

Jed said, "It was low when the picture was drawn. But trees grow. And that was a lot of years ago."

"Jed's right," said Liza. "We didn't think about that. How can we reach that hole?"

The children thought about this. Then Bill said, "There are three of us. Can't we lift somebody up for a look?"

"Good idea," said Jed.

"I guess I'm the one to be lifted," said Liza. "I'm the lightest."

"Do you mind?" asked Bill.

"Not as long as you don't drop me," said Liza.

"Don't worry," said Jed. "We won't let you fall. And you can hold onto the tree bark. It's rough enough to help you."

"Okay, Jed," said Bill. "You take one leg and I'll take the other. On the count of three, lift."

The boys boosted Liza up to the hole.

"Hurry up, Liza," said Bill. "You're heavier than I thought."

Liza started to stick her hand in the hole. Then she jerked it back.

"Let me down!" she screamed. "There's something furry in that hole."

Quickly the boys lowered her to the ground.

"What was it? What was it?" they asked.

"I think it was a raccoon. It had stripes around its tail."

"A raccoon!" said Jed.

"Do raccoons bite?" asked Bill.

"I don't know," said Jed. "But I wouldn't take a chance."

"What's he doing sleeping in the daytime?" asked Bill.

"Even I know the answer to that," said Liza. "Raccoons hunt at night and sleep during the day."

"So where does that leave us?" said Bill. "First a skunk, now a raccoon."

"We'll have to wait until after dark," said Jed.

"You mean we'll come tonight?" said Liza.

"Sure, why not?" said Bill. "The moon is usually bright and there's certainly nothing to hurt us."

"And I'll bet Hermit Dan sleeps at night," said Jed.

"Don't even mention that name," said Liza.

"Agreed," said Bill. "And when we come back we can bring a ladder."

"And hope that the raccoon is far away while we search his home."

"Talking about home," said Bill. "We might as well go back and take a swim."

"Yes," said Liza. "Gran should be there by now. Maybe she'll give me a lesson. I do so want to swim like her."

They started back for home. But they went quietly. They didn't want any dealings with Hermit Dan.

17

Midnight Prowl

The children changed into their swimsuits and went to the inlet. Grandpa had had his swim and was sitting in the sun. Gran was still in the water. She really loved swimming. Liza and Bill ran to join her. Jed turned toward Grandpa. He went over and flopped down.

"Grandpa," he said. "Do you know anything about seashells?"

"Not much," said Grandpa. "Are you interested in them?"

"Yes," said Jed. "I want to do a science project for next year."

"My brother was a bug about shells," said Grandpa. "He was quite a collector. Now wait a minute. Let me think."

Jed looked at Grandpa. A minute or so later, Grandpa said, "Yes, I'm sure we have that book still around. It's a great book on seashells with lots of colored pictures. I'll look it up for you."

"Thanks, Grandpa," said Jed. "That would be great."

Then Jed ran to join the others in the water.

Grandpa was as good as his word. He found the book for Jed. That afternoon Liza and Bill helped Gran make cookies. But Jed had begun his book and he chose to read. The book was old, but the pictures were beautiful. Jed made up his mind to learn more.

After supper the children were in Liza's room.

"All right," said Bill. "Does everybody know the plan?"

"Yes," said Liza. "But suppose we go to sleep? You know that happened to us once before."

"Don't worry," said Jed. "Go to sleep. I have my little alarm clock. I'm going to set it for midnight. I'll wake you up."

"That's good," said Liza. "Because I'm sleepy now."

"Why don't we go to bed early?" said Bill. "Then with a few hours' sleep we'll be ready to go."

"Good idea," said Jed. "We've had a busy day. I heard Gran tell Grandpa she wanted to go to bed early, too."

So the children got ready for bed as usual. They went down to say good-night to Gran and Grandpa.

"Early tonight, huh?" said Grandpa.

"We're tired," said Liza with a yawn.

"So am I," said Gran. "I'm ready for sleep myself."

Soon the whole house was quiet. Every Roberts was asleep.

Later Jed's alarm clock buzzed. He quickly turned it off. Then he tiptoed down the hall to wake Liza and Bill. Liza didn't want to wake up.

"All right," said Jed, "we'll go without you."

And that got Liza up.

In a few minutes they were dressed and slipping out of the house.

"Does everybody have a flashlight?" asked Bill.

"I do," said Jed.

"So do I," said Liza.

"All right then," said Bill. "Let's get that ladder."

The children had put the ladder at the edge of the woods before they went to bed. The boys picked it up.

"Okay, Liza," said Jed. "You put on your flashlight. We'll carry the ladder."

"All right," said Liza. She tried to turn on her flashlight. But nothing happened. She said, "Oh, no! My batteries must be dead."

"Well, that's a good start," said Jed. "Here, take mine."

Jed handed his flashlight to Liza. It had a bright clear beam.

"That's more like it," said Bill, "Okay, gang, it's merrily we march along."

The children set off into the woods. Everything looked strange. Shadows and darkness surrounded the children.

"Do you think this is all right?" asked Liza.

"Of course," said Bill. "Gran and Grandpa said it was safe here. We haven't ever heard a noise."

Just as he said that, they heard something crashing in the bushes. The children stopped. They

waited for something to happen. But nothing did.

"I guess we just scared an animal," said Jed.

"Not as much as it scared me," said Bill. "I think we should go back home."

"Go ahead," said Jed, "Liza and I are going to the initial tree."

Bill looked around. They were well into the woods now. He wasn't about to start back by himself.

"It is eerie," said Liza. "But let's just stick together. Nothing will happen. If we don't get to that raccoon's nest at night, we won't get the clue."

"Well, let's hurry," said Bill.

They hurried as much as they could and soon they reached the initial tree.

"Let me do the climbing," said Bill.

"The pleasure is all yours," said Liza, "unless Jed wants to do it."

"Go ahead, Bill," said Jed. "We'll hold the ladder."

Bill started up the ladder. He got to the hole. He reached into his pocket for his flashlight. No flashlight.

"Oh, no!" he said. "I lost my flashlight along the way."

"Some night," said Jed. "Here, take mine."

Jed handed his flashlight to Bill. Then he and Liza were nearly in the dark.

"Oh, do hurry, Bill," said Liza.

"Is the raccoon there?" asked Jed.

"No," called Bill. "All's clear, but I've got to clean out this hole a bit."

He began throwing out bark and twigs.

"Hey, take it easy," said Jed. "We're below. Be careful where you throw that stuff."

But Bill was too excited to hear. "I found it! I found it! It's another jar."

"Great-Uncle John had a thing about jars, didn't he?" said Liza.

Bill scrambled down the ladder. He said, "Let's open it now."

"Wait just a minute," said Jed. He took a stick and began digging in the soft earth.

"What are you doing?" asked Liza. "We've got the clue."

"I know," said Jed, "We're going to break the jar in this hole. Then we can cover the glass easily."

"Our practical brother," said Bill. He picked up a rock.

"Okay," said Jed. "The hole is ready. "I'll put the jar in."

Bill dropped the rock on it. The glass broke with the first hit.

"I see it! I see it!" said Liza. She knelt down to get the clue. "Oh," she said. "I cut myself."

"Is it bad?" asked Jed.

"No," said Liza. "It's just a little nick."

"Well, let me get the clue," said Bill. "You might bleed all over it."

He bent down and very carefully pulled out a rolled piece of paper. He unrolled it.

The other two looked over his shoulder.

"Another picture and no words!" said Liza.

"This one doesn't make any sense to me," said Jed. "But we'd better get back to the house with it. Remember, we only have one flashlight now."

"Liza, you take a turn at carrying the ladder," said Bill.

"All right," said Liza. "You take the flashlight."

The children started home. They were all silent. Their thoughts were on the new clue. What could it mean?

Suddenly there was a crash. Glass shattered.

The light disappeared. Liza and Jed stopped in their tracks.

"Bill!" they called.

"It's okay," said Bill. "I tripped."

"Are you hurt?" asked Liza.

"I don't think so," said Bill. "I twisted my ankle a little."

"Can you walk?" asked Jed.

"Yeah," said Bill. "It's not that bad."

"What about the flashlight?" said Liza.

Bill picked it up. He tried to turn it on. All he could get was a faint glow.

"That's not much better than nothing," said Liza. "Oh, Bill, why did you have to fall?"

"I couldn't help it," said Bill.

"Well, don't start fighting about it now," said Jed. "We shouldn't be too far from the house. It looks lighter up ahead. That must be the edge of the woods."

"Let's head for that spot," said Bill. "It's time we had one break tonight."

The children had to go more slowly and pick their way through the bushes. But finally they came to the edge of the woods. There it was light enough to see their way.

"Can't we leave the ladder here?" asked Liza.

"No," said Jed. "You know how Grandpa is. If we leave it, he'll want it first thing in the morning for sure."

So the children took the ladder back to the shed. Then they slipped indoors.

"Do we study the new clue tonight?" asked Bill.

"Not me," said Liza. "I just want to get back to bed. I feel cold and damp."

"Liza's right," said Jed, "If we put on a light Gran would be sure to see it. The clue can wait."

Bill yawned and said, "I can wait, too. What a night."

18

A Bloody Nose

Jed was the first of the three to wake up. He went to the kitchen. Gran and Grandpa were eating.

"Good morning, Jed," said Gran. "Get yourself some breakfast."

"Where are Liza and Bill?" asked Grandpa.

"Still asleep, I guess," said Jed.

"It will do them good," said Gran. "You three haven't stopped since you got here."

"They never do," said Grandpa. "I wonder if we ever had that much energy."

"I suppose we did at one time," said Gran.

"You don't do so badly now," said Jed. "You can swim longer than I can, Gran."

"That's not work for me," said Gran. "I learned to swim before I could walk."

"Liza swims well," said Jed.

"Yes," said Gran. "She's coming along nicely. I'm glad she wants me to teach her."

Jed finished his breakfast quickly. Then he said, "I'm going along the beach a little way."

"Seashells?" asked Grandpa.

"Yes," said Jed. "I want to see if I can find something different."

"Do you want us to tell Liza and Bill where you are?" asked Gran.

"Yes, please," said Jed. He went out the back door and ran down to the beach. It was low tide and there were a lot of shells on the beach. Jed started picking them up. But most of them he had already. Then he saw a different shell.

"Wow," he said. "That's a real find. I think a picture of it is in that seashell book."

He took his shell and ran back to the house. Liza and Bill were in the kitchen.

"We were just about to come and find you," said Bill.

"Where are Gran and Grandpa?" asked Jed.

"Oh, around, I guess," said Liza. "They told us where you were and left the kitchen. We just got our dishes cleaned up."

"Come on, Jed," said Bill. "We've got work to do."

"What work?" asked Jed. His mind was still on the seashell.

"The new clue," said Liza. "You didn't forget that, did you?"

"No," said Jed. "But there's something else I want to do first."

"Now what else could come before the clue?" said Bill.

"This," said Jed. "I want to look it up in the book. I don't know what kind it is."

"It's beautiful," said Liza. "May I hold it?"

Jed gave the shell to Liza. She studied it carefully. Then she gave it back to Jed.

"I wish you could find some more like that," said Liza. "They would make a beautiful bracelet."

"But the clue," said Bill. "It's more important than a stupid seashell."

"Who says so?" said Jed. "Maybe it's not more important to me."

"That seashell can wait," said Bill.

"So can the clue," said Jed.

Both boys were getting very angry. Suddenly Bill reached out and grabbed the shell. He threw it on the floor and stamped on it.

"There," he said. "That's how important your shell is."

Liza was horrified. The boys were glaring at each other. Suddenly Jed jumped on Bill. He threw him to the floor. The two boys began to fight it out.

"Help!" said Bill. "You're hurting me."

"I don't care," said Jed. "You deserve it."

He hit Bill in the nose. It began to bleed. The boys were screaming at one another.

Grandpa came running.

"What's all this about?" he asked. "Stop that fighting at once!"

But the boys didn't stop. Gran came in just as Grandpa was pulling them apart.

"Bill!" she said. "You're bleeding all over the kitchen floor. Liza, do get a cold cloth for his nose."

Liza ran to get the cloth.

The two boys stood there glaring at each other. Neither said a word.

"Did you see what happened, Liza?" asked Grandpa.

"Yes," said Liza. Then she stopped. How was she going to explain to Grandpa without telling him about the clue? Both boys looked at her.

"Well, would you please tell me what happened?" said Grandpa. "The boys don't seem ready to talk."

"It was like this," said Liza. "Jed found a beautiful shell on the beach. He wanted to look it up in the seashell book. Bill wanted him to do something else. But Jed wanted to find out about the shell first. Bill lost his temper. He grabbed the shell from Jed and stamped on it."

Then Liza began to cry. "And it was such a pretty shell, too."

She threw her arms around Gran. Gran let her cry. Grandpa looked at Bill.

"Is that the way it happened, Bill?" he asked.

Bill hung his head. He mumbled, "Yes, sir."

"That shell must have been pretty important to you, Jed," said Grandpa. "You usually find other ways to settle things."

Jed had tears in his eyes. He said, "It was, Grandpa. I never saw one like it."

He looked at the floor and said, "And there it is in little pieces. I may never find another one."

Then Bill began to sob. He ran to his room and closed the door. Grandpa put his hand on Jed's shoulder. He said, "I'm sorry this had to happen. Go wash up a bit. I'll talk to Bill."

Jed looked into Grandpa's eyes. He knew Grandpa understood. Jed said, "Thanks, Grandpa."

Jed went to his room and Grandpa went to talk to Bill.

"I'll clean up this mess, Gran," said Liza. "I need something to do after that."

"All right, dear," said Gran. She shook her

head, "Poor Bill, I wish he would learn to control his temper. It does get him into trouble. You've gotten better about controlling yours."

"I try, Gran," said Liza. "But sometimes mine gets me into trouble, too."

"Just keep on trying," said Gran. Then she chuckled, "You both come by it honestly. I had trouble when I was your age and your father was almost as bad as Bill."

"Really, Gran?" said Liza. "I never knew that."

"Oh, yes," said Gran. "Your Grandpa had many a talk with your father. He's probably saying the same things to Bill now."

Liza began to ask Gran more about when her father was a boy. Gran sat down. She told Liza some stories Liza hadn't heard before.

19

The New Clue

The children were soon friends again. Fight or no fight, they could not stay apart for long.

"Do you have the new clue, Liza?" asked Jed.

"Yes," said Liza. "It's in my room."

"I'm ready to work," said Jed. The three went into Liza's room. She got the clue.

"Boy," said Bill, "this one puzzles me completely."

"It's a hard one," said Jed.

"Well, let's find what we can," said Liza. "We know it's in the woods because of the trees."

"Yes," said Bill. "And there's a stream close by. The drawing shows that."

Jed was silent. The other two looked at him. They knew he was thinking about something. Suddenly his face lighted up.

"I've got it! I've got it!" he shouted.

"What!" said Liza and Bill.

"A cave!" said Jed. "Look at it closely. It can't be anything but a cave."

"A cave!" said Liza. She and Bill studied the picture.

"Say, you're right," said Bill.

"I do believe you are," said Liza. "But where on earth is there a cave?"

"In the woods," said Jed.

"By a stream," said Bill.

"Oh, stop it, you two," said Liza. "I'm serious. Where is this cave?"

"You've got me," said Bill.

"Somehow we'll have to find out from Grandpa," said Jed.

"Do you think you can do that, Liza?" asked Bill.

Liza thought about this. Then she said, "No, I think we should all do this."

"She's right," said Jed. "But we'd better make a plan. We can't be too obvious. You know we've already almost slipped up twice."

"We sure did," said Bill. "And, Liza, thanks for not telling when we got into that fight."

"Yes, Liza," said Jed. "You did real well. As angry as I was, I was afraid you'd tell."

"I almost did," said Liza. "That's why I took so long in getting started. But I figured that would make things worse. If Gran and Grandpa knew we were out at midnight they'd have a fit."

"But back to the cave," said Bill. "How do we go about finding out?"

The children thought about this. Liza said, "I know. Grandpa can't remember all the stories he's told us. Let's pretend he's told us about the cave. We can ask to hear the story again."

"Boy, you are a sneaky one," said Bill.

"But it's a good idea," said Jed. "And it just might work."

"Let's go find Grandpa," said Liza. "I think he's gone to the beach."

"We'd better change into our swimsuits," said Jed. "We have to make this look natural."

The children quickly changed. Then they told Gran where they were going.

They got to the beach just as Grandpa was coming out of the water.

"Good timing," said Bill to the others.

"And he'll be in a storytelling mood," said Jed. "He usually is after a swim."

"Hey, Grandpa," they called.

"Well," said Grandpa. "Company. I like that. Are you going for a swim or exploring the beach?"

"A little bit of everything," said Bill.

"Yes," said Liza. "We feel lazy today. We thought we'd come and talk you into telling us some stories."

"You always tell such good ones," said Jed. "We like to hear them over."

"Yes," said Liza. "You always remember something you haven't told us before."

"All right," said Grandpa. "It's a good day for storytelling. What kind of story would you like?"

The children pretended to think. Then Bill said, "About caves. If this is a pirate's island, there must be caves."

"That's a good idea," said Jed. "I like to hear about caves."

"Yes, Grandpa," said Liza. "Didn't you tell us about a cave here on the island?"

"I don't think so," said Grandpa. "At least, I don't remember."

"Maybe it was Dad who told us that one," said Jed.

"But there is a cave on the island, isn't there?" asked Bill.

Grandpa laughed and said, "You three do beat everything. I guess it was your father who told you. I was keeping it a secret. I wanted you to find it for yourselves."

The children could hardly cover up their excitement. They didn't know whether to push Grandpa any further or not. So they just waited. Finally Grandpa went on, "Yes, there is a cave. It's right by my fishing spot. But that's all I'm going to tell you. You'll have to explore until you find it yourselves."

"But tell us something about it," said Liza.

"Is it a pirate's cave?" asked Bill. "An honest-to-goodness pirate's cave?"

"I have no idea," said Grandpa. "We found it by accident. I doubt that it's a pirate's cave. Or, at least, there isn't any evidence of it."

"Does it have hiding places in it?" asked Jed.

"It is a hiding place," said Grandpa. "It has lots of little holes scattered around."

"Then it might be a pirate's cave after all," said Liza.

"You might be right," said Grandpa. "That will have to be for you to puzzle out. I'm sorry your father told you about it. I remember how much fun he had when he discovered it for himself."

"Did you go there much when you were a boy?" asked Liza.

"Oh, yes," said Grandpa. "It was a favorite picnic spot. We used to hide our lunch in the cave and explore all around. We liked exploring as much as you three do."

"Okay, then," said Jed. "If you won't tell us, that will be our project for the day."

"Sure," said Bill. "Let's ask Gran for a picnic lunch and take off."

"You'd better hurry," said Grandpa. "I know Gran is planning to come down here as soon as she gets through in the house."

"We're on our way," said Jed.

"Thanks, Grandpa," said Liza.

"I don't know what you're thanking me for,"

said Grandpa. "That wasn't much of a story. I have a feeling you three are up to something."

"We sure are," said Jed. "We're up to finding that cave."

Grandpa laughed. Bill said, "Come on, let's race to the house. Gran is a fast worker."

The three started to run.

20

Search for a Cave

The children caught Gran just in time. She let
them fix their own sandwiches. But she made
them a thermos of lemonade.

"That should do you for lunch," she said.
"Where are you off to?"

"To search for a cave," said Liza.

"Grandpa said we had to find it for ourselves,"
said Jed.

"You won't have much trouble," said Gran.
"Just head in the right direction."

"But what is the right direction?" asked Bill.

"As your Grandpa says," said Gran, "you'll have to find it for yourselves."

"Ahh," said the children.

Gran laughed and said, "I can't give away his secrets."

She went out the back door. The children took the lunch and went out after her.

"Now, think," said Jed. "Grandpa said it was near his fishing spot."

"He heads that way to go fishing," said Liza. "I saw him the other morning."

"Good," said Bill. "There must be a path or something. We'll follow it. Gran was right. This isn't going to be hard."

"Don't be too sure," said Jed. "These things always seem to get hard."

"We have to try it anyway," said Liza.

"Yeah," said Bill. "We'll never find it standing here."

The children headed in the direction Liza had said.

"You see," said Bill. "There *is* a path. All we do is follow it."

Bill was right. There was a path.

"Somebody else must like Grandpa's fishing

spot, too. This path looks as if it's used just about every day." said Jed.

"Hermit Dan!" said Liza. "Didn't Grandpa say he fished there?"

"He sure did," said Bill. "I hope we don't run into him today."

"It would spoil everything if we did," said Jed.

"I don't see why," said Bill. "This is Grandpa's property. And we're his grandchildren. That gives us some rights, doesn't it?"

"I don't think it does where Hermit Dan is concerned," said Jed.

"Oh, well. Let's not worry about that now," said Liza. "We'll see where the path leads."

The children walked along the path.

"Oh, oh," said Jed. "Here's the first trouble. The path divides. Which one should we take?"

"I vote to follow the way we're going," said Bill.

"That suits me," said Jed. "How about you, Liza?"

"Of course," said Liza. "I'm sure not going by myself."

The children walked on. Finally they saw an empty space ahead.

"Something tells me we chose wrong," said Jed.

"Yeah," said Bill. "There are trees around the cave."

"But there must be something here," said Liza.

The children walked on. Suddenly they stopped.

"A garden," said Liza. "Hermit Dan's garden."

There before them was a beautifully kept garden. And Hermit Dan was busily hoeing the rows.

"Don't let him see us," said Bill.

"No," said Jed. "Back down the path."

The children went partway down the path.

"Do we have to go all the way back?" asked Liza. "I know the cave is in this direction."

"No," said Jed. "We'll cut across. The underbrush isn't bad here."

The children started across the woods. Soon they heard the gurgling of water.

"There's a stream close by," said Liza. "I hear the water."

"And I see it," said Bill, running ahead.

"Let's see if we can find the source," said Jed. "I'm thirsty."

The children followed the stream to its source.

"Gee, it looks as if it just pours from that rock," said Bill.

"It sure does," said Liza. She scooped up a double handful and drank it.

"It's delicious," she said, "and icy cold."

All the children had drinks.

"We know the cave isn't far from here. We'll just follow the stream until we find it," said Jed.

The children walked along. Another stream seemed to join the first and it grew wider and deeper.

"We must be getting close to Grandpa's fishing place," said Bill.

"And closer to the cave, I hope," said Liza.

Then they saw it. It looked just like a hole in a rock.

"Gosh, I'll bet it's dark in there," said Bill. "Do we have a flashlight?"

"I think we broke all of them last night," said Liza. "I didn't think about the cave being dark."

"I did," said Jed. "And I brought along my other flashlight. But this time *I'm* going to hold it."

The children crawled into the cave. Once they

got through the hole, there was a large open space.

"Now for the search," said Bill. "Grandpa was right about there being all kinds of cubbyholes. I guess we'll have to look in all of them. Great-Uncle John didn't give any clue as to which one, did he?"

"Nope," said Jed. "And I looked carefully for that. We'll just have to poke in them all."

"But they're so dark," said Liza.

"And with one flashlight we can't see what we're doing," said Bill.

"You're right," said Jed. "It wouldn't be safe to just go sticking our bare hands in those holes."

"I know," said Liza. "Let's get some sticks. We'll stick them into the holes first. If there is anything alive there, it will run out."

"Good thinking," said Jed. "I'll get the sticks."

Jed did and soon the children were poking in all the holes. When nothing moved they thought it was safe to put their hands in. There seemed to be an endless number of holes to investigate. But finally Jed said, "I found something. I think I found it!"

"Is it another jar?" asked Bill.

"No," said Jed. "It's some kind of box."

"Come on," said Liza. "Let's get outside where we can really see."

The children left the cave. Jed held up a small metal box.

"Will it open?" said Bill.

Jed tried to open the box, but it would not give a bit.

"It must be rusted together or something," said Jed.

"Okay," said Bill. "Here's a good rock."

Jed handed him the box. Bill pounded on it. Soon it split apart. A piece of paper was inside the box.

Quickly Jed grabbed the paper and unfolded it. The children looked at it.

"It's two pictures," said Bill.

"We can see that," said Liza. "And the first one is of the house. But what does the second one mean? It looks like a small room."

"Does the house have an attic?" asked Jed. "That may be a secret room."

"Oh, come off it, Jed," said Bill. "Let's not get started with secret rooms."

"But this house may have one for sure," said Jed. "We'll have to think of some way to find out."

"Well, let's eat first. I'm starving," said Bill.

"So am I," said Liza. "Then we'll go back to the house and start looking."

21

The Round Window

The children ate their lunch by the stream.

"I wish I had a fishing rod," said Jed.

"There's one in the bushes," said Liza.

"Is it Grandpa's?" asked Bill.

"No," said Jed. "That's a pole. Grandpa has a rod."

"It must be Hermit Dan's!" said Liza. "Grandpa said he and Hermit Dan fished together. This must be Grandpa's fishing spot."

"Well, I'm not about to use it if it's Hermit

Dan's," said Jed. "But it would be fun to surprise Grandpa with some fish."

"I'll bet he wouldn't like that," said Liza.

"Why not?" asked the boys.

"He likes to think he's the only fisherman," said Liza. "And I think we should let him."

"It's all right with me," said Bill. "I don't like to feel live fish anyway, not even goldfish."

"And it's shells I'm interested in," said Jed.

"Well, I'm not about to touch a squirmy fish," said Liza. "So I guess Grandpa can be the fisherman."

The children walked home, exploring along the way. They got to the house just as Gran and Grandpa were finishing their lunch.

"Back so early?" asked Gran. "I thought you were gone for the day."

"Did you find the cave?" asked Grandpa.

"Yes," said Liza, "and I don't like it."

"Well, we liked it," said Grandpa. "We would take a lantern in and have great times."

"That's an idea," said Bill. "The next time we'll take a lantern. That will really light things up and make it more fun."

"By the way," said Grandpa. "Have you children gotten anywhere on my mystery?"

Grandpa caught the children by surprise. They didn't answer for a minute. Then Liza said, "We haven't seen a single red flower."

"I guess it is a bit early for those flowers," said Grandpa.

"Well, we have the whole summer," said Bill.

"Don't worry," said Jed. "We'll find your treasure for you."

"I would like that," said Grandpa. "I was thinking of trying to find it myself. Just haven't had time yet."

"Come on, gang," said Liza. "Let's go to my room."

The children left Gran and Grandpa talking.

"Wow!" said Bill. "That was a close one."

"Yes," said Jed. "Good thinking, Liza."

"Let's see what we can do with this new clue," said Bill.

Jed spread the paper out for them. There were two pictures on it.

One was of the outside of the house. An "x" was in a small round window. The other picture looked like a small room. It had a table and chair in it. On the wall were some squiggles that looked as if they might mean pictures. Under the chair was another small "x."

"This house *must* have an attic," said Liza. "I haven't seen any round windows.

"But I haven't seen any stairs either," said Bill.

"Maybe there's some other way to get to it," said Jed.

"I guess we'll have to ask Grandpa," said Liza.

"I'll tell you what," said Jed. "Let's go out front and look for the round window. Then we can tell him we noticed it and ask about an attic."

"That's a good idea," said Bill. "Come on, said Liza."

"Let me put the picture away first," said Liza.

She did that and followed the boys. They went out to the front of the house.

"Well, there really is a round window," said Bill. "I wonder why we never noticed it before?"

"Because we never use the front door," said Jed.

Just then Grandpa came around the house.

"What's so fascinating?" he asked.

"Oh, Grandpa," said Liza. "We were just looking at that top window. Does this house have an attic?"

"It sure does," said Grandpa.

"But I haven't seen any stairs to it," said Jed.

"No," said Grandpa. "There's a ladder contraption at the end of the hall. You have to pull it down to climb up."

"Can we go up there?" asked Bill.

"Sure," said Grandpa. "Just go to the end of the hall and you'll see what to pull."

"Do you want to go with us?" asked Liza.

"Thank you, no," said Grandpa. "I promised Hermit Dan I'd help him with something."

The children said nothing. They didn't even want to say Hermit Dan's name. Grandpa went on his way.

"What was that about?" asked Bill. "Asking Grandpa to go with us?"

"It wouldn't have looked right not to," said Liza.

"Liza's right," said Jed. "I just wish Gran would go someplace now."

No sooner had he said that than Gran called, "I'm going over to see the Widow Hawkins for a while."

"Have a good time," called Bill.

The children went into the house. They ran upstairs. There at the end of the hall was a loop of chain. Jed could just reach it. He pulled the chain and a ladder came down. Very quickly the three children were in the attic. They found themselves in a large square room with odd pieces of furniture here and there.

"This is the most cleaned-up attic I've ever seen," said Bill.

"It sure is," said Jed. "We could almost play basketball up here."

"Say, that's an idea!" said Bill.

"Come on, Bill," said Liza. "We are supposed to be solving a clue, not playing basketball."

"So what do we have to solve?" asked Bill.

"He's right, Liza," said Jed. "We need more information. Maybe we'd better study those pictures some more."

So the children were out of the attic much sooner than they expected. And they were no further along on their puzzle.

"We're missing something," said Jed.

"That's right," said Bill. "The whole solution to this clue."

"Oh, stop it, Bill," said Liza. "You know what Jed means."

"There's something in those pictures we're missing," said Jed. Then suddenly he said, "Hey, did you two see that round window in the attic?"

Liza and Bill looked surprised. Both said, "No!"

"That's it!" said Jed. "Let's study those pictures some more. I'm sure there is a secret room."

"Secret room, bah," said Bill.

"Oh, come off it, Bill," said Jed. "Just think about it, would you?"

"Oh, all right," said Bill.

"Do you see how the house goes out in the first picture?"

"Yeah," said Bill. "So what?"

"I see what you mean," said Liza. "The attic is square and it shouldn't be."

Bill perked up. He said, "Now I can see it. It should jut out where that round window that we didn't see is. Maybe there is a secret room."

"Right," said Jed.

"So it's back to the attic again," said Bill.

"No, wait a minute," said Jed. "Somebody get a hammer."

"I will," said Bill. "There's one in a kitchen drawer. Why do you need it?"

"You'll see," said Jed.

22

Excitement

Soon the children were back in the attic. This time they were more excited than the first time.

"All right," said Bill. "What's the hammer for?"

"I'll show you," said Jed. He walked over to the wall and began pounding it.

"Oh, I see," said Liza.

"Well, I don't," said Bill.

"He's trying to find where it's hollow," said Liza. "It will make a different sound."

Just then it did.

"Hey, that's it," said Bill. "You do have brains."

Jed continued pounding.

"That's it, all right," he said. "But what now?"

"If it's a room, there must be some way to get into it," said Liza.

"We could tear the wall down," said Bill.

"Oh, come on, Bill," said Jed. "Even secret rooms have doors or something. They are just hidden. Otherwise the rooms wouldn't be secret."

"So let's find the way to open it," said Bill.

The children began to search the hollow-sounding wall. They looked without success.

"I don't think we'll ever make this," said Bill. "Maybe we should call in Grandpa. He probably knows what this is all about."

"We may have to," said Jed. "But let's not yet. Look for anything that's different."

Suddenly Liza said, "Come here, boys. I found something that wiggles."

Both boys moved to where she was.

"See if you can get the hammer into that hook," said Liza.

"I can get my finger under it," said Bill.

He did just that and pulled. A door opened into a small room.

"By gosh, we found it," said Bill.

"And it's just like the picture," said Jed. "There's the table and the chair and the pictures on the wall are seashells. It just has to be Great-Uncle John's room."

"The other 'x' was under the table," said Liza.

"Then let's move it and find the secret," said Bill.

The children quickly moved the table. Then they began to search the floor. "Isn't that a small chain almost in that floorboard crack?" asked Liza.

Jed looked where she pointed. He touched the small links. Then he put his finger through them. He started to pull.

"Wait," said Liza.

"Wait for what?" asked Bill.

"I heard Gran and Grandpa come in," said Liza. "Shouldn't they be here now?"

The children looked at one another.

"You're right," said Jed. "I think we should call them."

Liza went to the top of the stairs. She called, "Gran, Grandpa, come quickly. Come up to the attic."

"The attic!" said Gran. "Whatever for?"

"It's important," said Liza.

She heard Gran say, "Now what are those children up to?"

"I don't know, but we had better see," said Grandpa.

"Come on," said Liza.

"Just be patient," said Gran. "We're coming."

The children were almost jumping with excitement.

Gran and Grandpa came into the attic. The first thing Grandpa said was, "I see you've found my brother's secret room. How did you ever get into it? Mary and I never could. It was John's secret place and we could only go in by invitation. We never knew how to open the door."

The children stared at Grandpa. Bill said, "You mean, you really didn't know how to get in?"

"No," said Grandpa. "My father built it for my brother so he could have a place away from us. You see, we thought he was the greatest and wanted to tag along with him all the time. He wanted to study shells for these pictures. So he asked Dad for a place that was off-limits for us unless he invited us. My dad understood and built this room for him."

The children showed Grandpa how to open the door.

Then Jed said, "But that's not the big surprise."

"You mean you found something else?" asked Gran.

"Just wait and see," said Liza. "Ready, Jed?"

"Ready," said Jed.

He pulled off the top of the hiding place. Grandpa shouted, "My ship! Look at that, Gran. And I never knew about that cubbyhole!"

Very carefully he lifted the ship out of its hiding place.

"I never thought I'd see that again. I did a good job on it," he said.

"You sure did, Grandpa," said Bill.

"Oh, do hurry," said Liza. "Get the other things out."

Jed pulled out a box. He opened it. There were two small tissue-wrapped packages. He opened them.

"Oh, oh," he said. "I'm afraid these are ruined. It's the pin and the buckle, but they're all black."

"Nonsense," said Gran. "That's just tarnish. A little polish and they will be as good as ever."

"Where's the needlepoint bag?" asked Liza.

Jed pulled out another box. He said, "Maybe this is it. Here, you open it."

Liza opened it and took out a beautifully made drawstring bag.

"Oh, it's beautiful," she said. "I wish Aunt Mary was here."

Gran put her arms around her. She said, "Don't feel sad. Aunt Mary is here in our memories. I'm sure she would want you to have the bag. She had no children, and you are her oldest grand-niece. She loved you."

Liza looked up and smiled. She said, "Thanks, Gran."

"Is that all?" asked Grandpa.

"I'm trying to see," said Jed. "No, it looks like

there is a big flat box under here, too."

He pulled it out. Grandpa said, "It's John's seashell collection! I would know that box anywhere."

Jed lifted off the top. For minutes the family was silent. Then Liza said softly, "It's gorgeous."

"I was just thinking that," said Jed.

"Well, for once, John was right. He may have taken the things we most liked. But he also took the thing he most liked," said Grandpa.

"Grandpa," said Jed. "Look at this. He had a book and had written about each shell."

"Yes," said Grandpa. "That collection was one thing he was serious about. He polished each shell himself and found out all he could about each one."

"Wow!" said Jed. "I wish I knew that much."

"You can," said Grandpa. "I think your Uncle John would have wanted you to have the collection."

Then Grandpa turned to Bill. He said, "And I want you to have my ship model."

There were no words to say. They all felt very close to each other at that moment. Each took his treasure and silently they left the attic.

Later that day, Grandpa said, "And just this

morning I asked you if you were getting anywhere with my mystery.''

"But we didn't say 'yes' or 'no,' " said Liza.

"What did we say, anyway?" said Bill.

"We just said we hadn't seen any red flowers,"
said Liza.

Grandpa threw back his head and laughed.
Gran joined in.

"They're right," she said. "That's just what Liza
said."

"I'll never get used to the way they turn things
on me," said Grandpa.

Bestselling books by

Beverly Cleary

☐ BEEZUS AND RAMONA	40665-X	$3.25
☐ CUTTING UP WITH RAMONA!	41627-2	$3.95
☐ DEAR MR. HENSHAW	41794-5	$3.25
☐ ELLEN TEBBITS	42299-X	$3.25
☐ EMILY'S RUNAWAY IMAGINATION	42215-9	$3.25
☐ GROWING UP FEET (Young Yearling)	40109-7	$3.95
☐ HENRY AND BEEZUS	43295-2	$3.25
☐ HENRY AND RIBSY	43296-0	$3.25
☐ HENRY AND THE CLUBHOUSE	43305-3	$3.25
☐ HENRY AND THE PAPER ROUTE	43298-7	$3.25
☐ HENRY HUGGINS	43551-X	$3.25
☐ JANET'S THINSANAJIGS (Young Yearling)	40108-9	$3.95
☐ MITCH AND AMY	45411-5	$3.25
☐ THE MOUSE AND THE MOTORCYCLE	46075-1	$3.25
☐ OTIS SPOFFORD	46651-2	$3.25
☐ RALPH S. MOUSE	47582-1	$3.25
☐ RAMONA AND HER FATHER	47241-5	$3.25
☐ RAMONA AND HER MOTHER	47243-1	$3.25
☐ RAMONA, FOREVER	47210-5	$3.25
☐ RAMONA, QUIMBY, AGE 8	47350-0	$3.25
☐ RAMONA THE BRAVE	47351-9	$3.25
☐ RAMONA THE PEST	47209-1	$3.25
☐ THE REAL HOLE (Young Yearling)	47521-X	$3.95
☐ RIBSY	47456-6	$3.25
☐ RUNAWAY RALPH	47519-8	$3.25
☐ SOCKS	48256-9	$3.25
☐ TWO DOG BISCUITS (Young Yearling)	49134-7	$3.95

At your local bookstore or use this handy page for ordering:

DELL READERS SERVICE, DEPT. DYA
P.O. Box 5057, Des Plaines, IL. 60017-5057

Please send me the above title(s). I am enclosing $_____.
(Please add $2.00 per order to cover shipping and handling.) Send
check or money order—no cash or C.O.D.s please.

Ms./Mrs./Mr._____

Address _____

City/State_____ Zip _____

DYA–12/89

Prices and availability subject to change without notice. Please allow four to six
weeks for delivery.